Katie's Big Match

Mr Brownfield plugged the final as well, and said he was sure everyone would agree that such a successful team deserved a proper kit. Katie looked round and saw that the boy's team were looking green. There was a noticeable lack of admiring announcements about *them* in assembly at the moment. Katie, nudging Megan to point out the positively demonic expression on Max's face, felt a nervous shiver wriggle down her spine. *Obviously* she wasn't scared (of that lot?!) but she had a feeling that the boys were going to be doing whatever it took to win. . .

Look out for lots more stories about the triplets:

Becky's Terrible Term
Annabel's Perfect Party
Becky's Problem Pet

Holly Webb

Triplets

Katie's Big Match

SCHOLASTIC

Scholastic Children's Books,
Commonwealth House, 1–19 New Oxford Street,
London, WC1A 1NU, UK
a division of Scholastic Ltd
London ~ New York ~ Toronto ~ Sydney ~ Auckland
Mexico City ~ New Delhi ~ Hong Kong

Published in the UK by Scholastic Ltd, 2004

Copyright © Holly Webb, 2004

ISBN 0 439 97341 4

Printed and bound by Nørhaven Paperback A/S, Denmark

2 4 6 8 10 9 7 5 3 1

Chapter One

"Come on, come on, come on – yeeeeeesssss!" Becky and Mum leaped up and down and cheered as Manor Hill scored another goal. Or to be precise, *Katie* scored another goal. It was Katie's first game for the team, and Mrs Ross, the junior team coach, was looking like the cat that got the cream. Putting Katie Ryan up front had *definitely* been a good idea.

Annabel was decidedly less enthusiastic about the whole thing. "So that was good then, was it?" she muttered gloomily.

Becky and Mum glared at her.

"Anna*bel*!" said Becky disgustedly. "You know perfectly well that was a goal – Katie's *second* goal. You're just being stupid. I mean, I'm not that into football either, but it's so exciting! Katie's brilliant at this! Look, the other team's coach looks as though she

1

could quite happily tear Katie into little bits and jump on them," she concluded bloodthirstily, beaming happily at the seething coach, who actually looked as though Katie's identical triplets were on her tearing and stomping list as well.

"But it's so co-old. . ." moaned Annabel. "And I'm hungry, and my feet hurt. Couldn't we have brought chairs?" she suddenly appealed to Mum.

"Annabel, the sun is shining, it's only October, and you are wearing a jacket, a scarf, a hat and *mittens*, for heaven's sake! And you've only been standing for half an hour," said Mrs Ryan in response.

Annabel surveyed her outfit happily – it was the only thing bearable about this boring afternoon. A mind-numbingly tedious Geography lesson (somehow always worse on a Friday, impossible though that might seem) and now being forced to watch *football*. She stroked the tassels of her cream-and-pink-striped scarf against her cheek, then tugged the matching hat closer round her ears and shivered dramatically for Mum's benefit. Of course, there was no way she'd have missed Katie's first football match, but she was going to make sure that everybody appreciated her being there as much as possible. Especially as she had some serious beginning-of-the-weekend lounging around the house and blatantly not doing her homework to get on with.

Annabel turned her attention back to the muddy pitch, where Katie's best friend Megan was about to face her first real challenge. It was Megan's first game for the Manor Hill team as well, and she'd been a bit nervous. Katie and Megan were in Year Seven, but most of the team was made up of Year Eights – a couple of whom had been lazy about turning up to practice recently, and Mrs Ross had *very* definite feelings about that. If you missed practices for no good reason, you didn't get to play, even if it was the league quarter-final. But there had been some sulky muttering among the Year Eights: how come these three Year Seven players had managed to get on to the team in their first year at Manor Hill?

The third new Year Seven player was Cara Peters, which was the only thing taking the shine off it all for Katie. Cara was one of her least favourite people at school – she was one of Amy Mannering's two best

friends, and Amy Mannering was the triplets' arch-
enemy. Katie couldn't deny that Cara was good, though.
In fact, Cara was nearly as good as she was, even though
it was torture to admit it. Cara and Katie were both
natural strikers, and serious competition for each other. It
was just a pity that Cara was a natural brat as well.

Megan was facing her first major challenge of the
game. She was goalie, and up till now most of the action
had been up the other end of the pitch as Katie and Cara
put on a brilliant display and pretty much dazzled the
Hillcrest defence. But now the fierce-looking Hillcrest
captain with boyishly short black hair was racing down
the field towards Megan with a very grim look on her
face. She was seriously fast, and the Manor Hill defence
had been resting on its laurels a bit, and been taken by
surprise. Now it was the Hillcrest supporters who were
holding their breath, and their cross-looking coach had
both fists tightly clenched as she watched the black-
haired girl getting closer and closer to what would
hopefully be their first goal of the match.

Becky, Mum and even Annabel watched anxiously.
They liked Megan a lot, and Katie had told them how

nervous she was about her first game. It was such a responsibility playing in goal – especially with eight rather hostile twelve year olds just waiting for you to slip up. Megan didn't *look* worried, though. In fact, now that she had something to do she looked eager, and determined – just as determined as the Hillcrest girl, who was about to take her shot.

Katie reckoned that Megan could actually read minds. How else was it that eight times out of ten she knew which way you were going, and had her gloves in just the right place? When they were practising in the park Megan seemed to know where Katie was putting the ball before Katie did. Certainly she looked pretty confident now. The Hillcrest striker took her shot. The ball sailed towards Megan and she dived expertly to the right. A save! Megan hugged the ball as though she never meant to let it go.

"Yaaaay! Go, Megan!" came a particularly loud cheer – it was all three triplets, yelling completely as one. Several of the other supporters looked quite disconcerted. Megan was grinning hugely as she booted the ball back up the field. It hadn't been a very difficult save, but it had looked great! Her dad was beside himself, bouncing around all over the place and chortling, nudging her mum and pointing out how well Megan had done, while Megan's mum patiently agreed with him.

Becky suddenly felt really sorry for Katie. Their dad should be here, too! Two goals in her first game was absolutely fantastic, and there was no way he'd ever really be able to know what it was like, even though Mum had taken loads of photos. She felt quite cross with Dad all of a sudden – why did he have to work so far away? Megan's dad had obviously taken time off work, but their dad wasn't going to be popping back from Egypt to watch Katie, even if Manor Hill went all the way to the final. She wondered if Katie felt the same way.

Neither team scored in the second half, so it was a jubilant Manor Hill side who romped off the field at full-time. Three–nil! And Hillcrest were a good team. Katie and Megan came over to the sidelines to be congratulated, looking very pleased with themselves. Katie was looking hopeful, too. "Mum, I don't suppose Megan could come back for tea? If that's all right with you too, Mrs Jones?" she added politely.

Mrs Ryan looked distant for a moment, and the triplets waited patiently. It wasn't that Mum was annoyed, she was just trying to remember what they were having for tea and whether there was enough of it. Finally, she smiled. "That would be fine –" she turned to Megan's parents – "if it fits in with your plans? In fact, if you wanted, Megan could stay the night. The girls are all going into town shopping tomorrow, aren't they?"

"Ooooh, yes! Please, Mum, that would be fab!" Megan pleaded.

"Well, if you're sure it's no trouble. What clothes do you want for tomorrow, Meg?" asked Mrs Jones. "We'll nip home and then your dad'll run them across for you." Then she looked Megan and Katie up and down and grinned. "You sure you've got enough hot water, Sue? These two look like they've been playing in a swamp, not a field."

"Might as well be," said Katie disgustedly. "The goals are like soup."

So it was settled – Megan was sleeping over. She and the triplets raced for the car. There was a brief delay while Mrs Ryan covered every centimetre of upholstery that might possibly come into contact with Katie or Megan in newspaper, and then they headed home.

The tea that Mrs Ryan had been trying to remember was pasta with tomato sauce, and there was plenty to go round, including loads of yummy cheese to melt on top. Katie and Megan were too excited to concentrate much on what they were eating, though. They couldn't believe that they'd won their first match! And not only that, it had been the quarter-final.

"This is only Manor Hill's second year in the schools league," Katie explained to the others, stabbing her fork at Mum for emphasis. "Last year we came absolutely *nowhere*, 'cause Mrs Ross had only just started up the team and they were useless, everyone says so. But if we win the next match, we'll be in the *final*!"

"Oh no!" exclaimed Annabel dramatically. "Does that mean I have to go to *another* football match?"

"Will you definitely get to play?" asked Becky anxiously. It would be awful if Katie and Megan got demoted back to subs again.

Katie looked thoughtful. "What do you reckon, Megan?" she asked her friend, who now had a tomatoey ring round her mouth to match her red hair.

"I'm just not sure." Megan sounded frustrated. "Mrs Ross told Caroline and Michelle and Lizzie that they'd be back on the team if they put the effort in, but from what the others were saying, I don't think they're that bothered. Got better things to do, I suppose." Megan shrugged, as though she really couldn't imagine what.

"I don't see how Mrs Ross could stop you playing after today," said Becky stubbornly, sticking up for her triplet. "I mean, two goals! And you pulled off some brilliant saves, Megan," she added, smiling.

"Yeah, they were fab, especially that one that you dived for. And Cara scored as well," Katie pointed out gloomily, "so we're not getting rid of her either. We'll just have to hope that Mrs Ross thinks we're the best thing for the team. And that Cara breaks her leg," she added with a grin. Then she had a sudden thought. "Mum, can I ring Dad? To tell him about the match? I know it costs loads, but I'll pay for it out of my pocket money. Please?"

Mum smiled at her. "Dad's waiting for you to call. He e-mailed this morning to check he had the right day. Don't forget to give the others a chance to talk too, though."

Katie danced over to the counter to get the phone. "You don't mind, do you, Megan?"

Megan shook her head. "Course not."

Katie dialled, and Dad must have been waiting by the phone, because he picked up immediately, and Katie burst into excited chatter. "We won, Dad! I scored two goals, and now we're in the semi-final!" She'd pressed the speakerphone button, so they all heard his reply.

"Fantastic! Well done, sweetheart! I knew you could do it."

Then they went all technical, so the others decided to have second helpings until Katie and her dad had stopped discussing footwork, and they could talk about

10

"normal stuff". It took quite a long time, but at last Katie passed the phone over to Becky and Annabel, who both huddled over it at the same time, and sat back down at the kitchen table.

"More pasta, Katie?"

"Mmmm." Katie took seconds, and proceeded to push the pasta round her plate. Somehow, telling Dad about her triumphant game, and hearing how excited he was, had made her miss him loads – telling him all about it had been brilliant, but she really wished she hadn't needed to. . .

That night, Megan slept on an inflatable mattress in-between the triplets' beds. She and Katie were exhausted after the match (and the twenty minutes of mad puffing it had taken to blow up the mattress) but they were pretty hyper as well, so there was quite a bit of hysterical giggling at things that really weren't all that funny, before Megan suddenly shut up mid-sentence, and had obviously fallen asleep. Becky and Annabel were half-snoozing already (there was only so much fantasy football team-picking they could take) so only Katie was left awake.

She was feeling odd. It had been a brilliant day (two goals! She still couldn't believe it!) but something was not right, and she was pretty sure she knew what it was. She loved Megan loads – she was the first really close friend Katie'd had apart from her sisters, but at 4.42 that afternoon she hadn't liked her much. And that was making her feel really really mean. Katie hadn't been able to help it, though. She'd been cheering Megan's fab save and heard Becky and Annabel yelling too. She'd turned to wave at them and there he was – dancing around like he'd won the lottery – Megan's dad. It was so unfair. No, it was worse than unfair, it was wrong. Why was Megan's dad there to go crazy about a stupid save when *her* dad was in *Egypt*? Katie wasn't really a crying person – she reckoned that Becky had got Katie's share of crybabyness as well as her own – but now she could feel a choking lump in her throat that meant she really wanted to cry. Or, preferably, scream. And shout. Lots. And she wouldn't mind kicking something either – Dad maybe.

Katie sniffed, and sighed, and turned over with a huffy thump, snuggling the duvet around her shoulders. She didn't need Dad there for everything. That was stupid. She had Mum, and she had Becky and Annabel, and they were like having something infinitely better than sisters (and worse, sometimes). This afternoon Annabel had watched an entire football match, and she'd only moaned about it every other sentence for the rest of the evening – for Annabel that was serious sisterly devotion. No, Katie would be fine without Dad. She was making a big fuss about nothing. But as she finally drifted off to sleep, all she could see was one amazingly perfect afternoon in the garden, just before her parents split up. She and Dad playing football, very carefully avoiding the rug where Becky and Annabel were sitting playing with the guinea pigs. Or rather, arguing about whether Annabel could give Maisy a furcut so she could actually see. Dad was cheering – the ball had definitely gone between the two rose bushes – Katie had scored a goal. . .

Chapter Two

"Annabel! Bel, come on, wake up. Come on, we've got to have breakfast before we go and meet the others, get up!"

"There's no point telling her like that, Katie," said Becky, while Megan looked on blearily from her sleeping bag. "This is the only way – watch. Ann-a-bel, Ann-a-bel . . . shopping. . ." she cooed.

Annabel sat bolt upright in bed immediately, and the other three howled with laughter, which infuriated her completely. "What? What is it? Have you done something to my hair?" She rounded suspiciously on Katie.

"No, honestly, Bel. We were just laughing because you sat up so fast – hey, where are you going? *I'm* going in the bathroom first! Bel! Oh, no!" Katie turned back from glaring at the bedroom door and the vanishing flash of pink pyjamas that was Annabel. Becky's magic word had woken her up way too fast. "We may as well go and get some breakfast," she sighed. "She's going to be ages."

"Your mum won't mind us having breakfast in our pyjamas?" asked Megan, standing up and bringing her sleeping bag with her.

Katie shrugged off the remnants of last night's strange crossness with Megan, and shook her head. "Nope, not at the weekend. She'll probably be wearing hers. Are you doing a caterpillar impression or something?"

"I'm doing a not-awake-person impression," yawned Megan. Then she seemed to perk up a bit. "Hey, I've just thought! Have you ever sledged downstairs in a sleeping bag?"

Katie and Becky looked at her as though she'd sprouted whiskers.

"No, really, it's brilliant. I'll show you." Megan shuffle-hopped out of the bedroom to the top of the stairs. "You two go down to the bottom and watch," she directed. She waited until Becky and Katie were in place at the bottom of the stairs, then she sat down on the top step and started to wriggle inside her sleeping bag. She started to slide, her padded sleeping bag cushioning her over each bump. Gradually she picked up speed, until her excited squeaks at each bump became one long squeak, and she ended up at the bottom of the stairs in a giggling heap. By this time Becky and Katie had realized that Megan wasn't as mad as they'd suspected – in fact, she might just have let them in on a brilliant new game.

"That's so cool!" said Katie. And then she added triumphantly, "And that's my sleeping bag, so I'm definitely having next go!"

Megan obligingly wormed her way out of the sleeping bag, and Katie raced up to the top of the stairs. By the time Annabel came out of the bathroom looking smug and positively glowing with cleanliness, she was rather annoyed to find that they hadn't minded her clever queue-jumping tactics at all. She refused point-blank to get into "Katie's smelly sleeping bag" and have a go, but then Katie demonstrated for her and she decided she definitely didn't want to be left out. It was a good ten minutes later when they finally trooped into the kitchen for breakfast. Mum had been sitting at the kitchen table sipping coffee and shuddering every time there was a particularly loud thump. She knew exactly what they'd been doing – her parents' house had a spiral staircase, and she and her twin sister, the triplets' Auntie Janet, had raced down it in sleeping bags when they were about the triplets' age. At least this lot seemed to be sticking to one at a time. . .

"Hello!" Mum looked them all up and down with interest. "Oh good, you *are* still in one piece. I did wonder."

"Mum, Megan showed us the best game, it's so funny, you'll never guess what we've been doing!" gabbled Annabel.

"Sweetheart, I know exactly what you've been doing – if I didn't, don't you think I'd have come running when I heard you hurling yourselves down the stairs? It sounded like an avalanche out there. Is the sleeping bag still usable?"

Annabel sulked over to join the others, getting juice at the fridge. "I knew it – Mum's got a security camera on those stairs. How else could she know?" she muttered crossly, as her mother smiled to herself behind their backs.

The triplets and Megan settled themselves around the big pine kitchen table with bowls of cereal to take the edge off their hunger. Mum always made something special for breakfast at the weekends. She got up and put the grill on – "Bacon sandwiches for everybody?"

There was a general chorus of yes-type noises made though mouthfuls of cereal, except for Megan, who swallowed fast and managed to say, "That would be lovely, Mrs Ryan," in a very polite voice before she choked and disappeared under three people thumping her on the back.

☆　❀　♡

Half an hour later everyone was still sitting round the table, sleepily licking bacon and ketchup off their fingers, when Annabel looked at the clock, and sat up straight. "What time are we meeting the others?"

Becky squinted thoughtfully at the clock. "Ummm, at the end of the road . . . twenty-seven minutes from now?"

By the time she'd finished her sentence, Katie, Annabel and Megan were already on the stairs, and she was talking to an empty table.

Mum grinned at her. "I'd say the chances of you getting in the bathroom this morning are pretty low."

"No, it's OK, Bel's already washed. . ." yawned Becky, sleepily heading for the stairs.

Believe it or not, twenty-seven minutes later Megan and the triplets were, if not actually at the end of the road, at least within waving distance of Fran and Saima. Annabel looked glossily perfect in a denim skirt, bright pink tights and her current favourite things, her silver Kickers boots (bought with several months' pocket money). She'd even had time to curl her hair. The other three looked fine but not up to her standards, and Annabel was doing Becky's hair as they jogged along. Becky had thought her hair looked perfectly OK, but Annabel said she wouldn't be seen dead with someone whose hair looked like that.

The six of them squashed on to the bench at the bus stop, chattering happily. Megan and Katie passed on the good news about yesterday's match, and then they got down to the important business of which shops they were going to that morning. They were going into Stallford, the big town that they all lived on the outskirts of. Darefield had its own high street with a couple of nice shops (including a brilliant clothes shop called Silver) but for serious shopping, they needed to go into town. On the top deck of the bus they worked out the plan of campaign.

"TopShop, obviously," said Saima, who was as clothes-mad as Annabel, and currently a lot richer, having not spent what both her mother and sisters considered a ridiculous amount of money on silver boots.

"Oh, *obviously*," grinned Katie, but she was only teasing. "And, let me guess, Claire's Accessories and GirlStuff. Why are we even bothering to talk about it?"

"Well, where do *you* want to go?" asked Annabel in a very patient, talking-to-a-dim-person sort of voice.

"I don't mind those places – as long as we go to a couple of sports shops as well, and you and Saima don't moan all the time. What about you, Becky?"

"Don't mind." Becky shrugged, and shot an enquiring

glance at Fran. "Can we go to the pet shop? We could always split up if it's only me and Fran who want to."

"Don't be silly," said Katie firmly. "We go to the pet shop for you two, the sports shop for me and Megan and clothes shops so Bel can drool while Saima buys stuff. More fun that way than splitting up. OK?"

Everyone nodded – Katie was very good at taking charge, but she did tend to get things sorted, so it was easier just to let her get on with it.

"But GirlStuff first 'cause it's closest to the bus stop, OK?" added Saima.

GirlStuff sold everything – clothes, shoes (it was where the silver boots had come from), hair stuff, make-up. Saima and Annabel probably could have spent all day in there, if the others hadn't got bored after half an hour and started sighing every time they picked up something new. Saima bought a pair of black tights with big pink flowers on and got huffily upset when Katie seemed to find them hilariously amusing.

"I'm sorry, Saima, they're very – sweet, it's just *funny*, great big flowers all over your legs—" Here Annabel trod on her foot, and she shut up.

"They're gorgeous, Saima, Katie just has no taste. Come on, let's go. Hey, what are Becky and Fran buying?" Annabel sounded slightly amazed – this was an Annabel and Saima shop. It turned out that the same range of tights also had a purple pair with cute, slinky little black cats on, which Becky had fallen in love with.

"We'd better get Katie to a sports shop before she explodes," said Saima, grinning. She was a very sweet-natured person, and her huff about the tights had been more for the principle of the thing than because she really minded.

Megan and Katie were perfectly capable of spending hours in a sports shop, so after a quick wander around, and ten minutes of looking at very cool and unbelievably expensive trainers, Annabel, Saima, Becky and Fran came over to where Megan and Katie were, and perched themselves on the edge of a skiwear display to wait. The shop was packed, and the assistants were far too busy to care – at least, that was what Annabel told Becky very firmly when she dithered about whether it was OK to sit there or not. "Besides, I'm exhausted. Oh, Becky, sit down, you look as though you're about to stick a pair of skis down your jumper, and that'll bring that spotty boy over here if nothing else will. Sit!"

Becky sat, and the four of them turned their attention to Megan and Katie, who were sadly surveying the football stuff. Racks and racks of super-expensive team shirts, celebrity-endorsed boots, and towering piles of gleaming footballs. Katie and Megan looked depressed, and distinctly envious of a couple of boys who were trying on boots.

"What's the matter?" asked Saima, looking puzzled. "Can't you afford anything?"

Katie came over. "Nope," she said, chewing the end of her ponytail. "It's all way too much. I mean, look—"

"I know what I meant to ask you. Those shirts reminded me," burst out Annabel suddenly. "Why doesn't your football team have proper shirts? I mean, like those other girls had?"

Katie sighed. It was true – the Hillcrest side had been wearing neat black shorts and shirts quartered in black and purple. They had purple blazers too, so she supposed the strip matched their uniform. The Manor Hill girls just wore their green PE shorts and white polo shirts – it didn't look like a proper team outfit.

Megan had given up sighing over the Manchester United shirts and joined them in time to hear Annabel's question. She made a face. "I know, it isn't fair. But the team's only been playing since last year, and there hasn't been any money for us to have a special strip."

"But the boys have one, don't they?" Fran sounded confused. "I'm sure they do, I've seen that idiot Max wearing it – a red shirt?"

"Yup." Now Katie scowled. "The boys' team's been going for ages. I don't think there's any money for us to have special shirts made."

There was silence as everyone digested the unfairness of this.

"Are the boys' team any good?" asked Becky eventually.

"Nope," and "They're OK," said Katie and Megan at the same time.

Katie shrugged. "Like Fran said, Max is in the team. I

suppose they're all right, but *no way* are they as good as us."

"That's so not fair." Annabel sounded really cross. Football might be deeply boring as far as she was concerned, but she knew Katie was a brilliant player, and it seemed totally out of order that she shouldn't have all the stuff she needed.

"Come on." Katie heaved Annabel up off the ski display. "Hanging about here's just going to make me and Megan all huffy. And that spotty guy's giving us a funny look."

"Seriously, though," continued Annabel as they left the shop, walking past the spotty sales assistant and smiling sweetly at him, "you *should* have the proper kit. It didn't look good, just wearing your PE shirts. Like you couldn't be bothered."

"Don't tell me," snapped Katie irritably. "Tell the school!" But she smiled at Annabel to take the edge off her words, and then changed the subject. "OK. Pet shop? Are we just bunny-gazing, or are you actually buying something, Becky?"

That was the end of it for the moment – even

Annabel could see that Katie and Megan were annoyed and it wouldn't be fair to keep on about it – but Katie couldn't dismiss the idea as easily as she pretended. The whole time that Becky and Fran stood in front of a cage of black-and-white rats looking lovestruck, while Saima and Annabel shuddered theatrically and made hissing comments about the plague, she seethed to herself at the unfairness of it. Even a litter of kittens, which sent all six of them into fits of "aaah"ing, couldn't completely get football shirts out of Katie's head. And they, and Dad, stayed at the back of her mind for the rest of the weekend.

Chapter Three

After their shopping expedition on Saturday, the triplets spent the rest of the weekend loafing around, and doing the totally unreasonable amount of homework that they'd been set. Shopping wore you out! Katie loafed and grumped at the same time, but after a whole day and a half of growling quietly about how unfair it was that Manor Hill wouldn't pay for their team to have a real football strip, she got bored with herself. If there wasn't the money, then there wasn't the money, and what was the point of moaning about it? She knew perfectly well that there were times when going on (and on and on) about something would get it for you – she and Becky and Annabel had it down to a fine art. (When you whined in triplicate, you were practically irresistible.) But this was *not* one of them. So being Katie, she decided to do something about it herself instead. She was pretty sure that Mrs Ross, their coach, and the rest of the PE staff would be delighted if the girls' team had their own shirts – they couldn't much like the scruffy look of the girls when they were playing matches against smartly turned-out teams like Hillcrest. It made *everyone* look as though they weren't taking the team seriously. So, really, it was just the money that was the problem.

Katie was very silent at breakfast on Monday – having worked this conclusion through in her mind, she wasn't entirely sure where to go next. How much did football shirts even *cost*, anyway? She had a feeling that the team might have to buy quite a lot of them because they'd always be getting lost, or torn, or shrunk by people's parents who accidentally put things in the washing machine at boil-wash temperatures. It wouldn't work to make people just buy a shirt when they joined the team, mused Katie to herself, sucking on her spoon with an expression of total idiocy that sent Annabel into hysterics – although Katie took no notice of her whatsoever. No, that wouldn't be fair. People already had to get their own boots. What if somebody was really good at football, but just couldn't afford the shirt? It might put them off totally.

Katie got this far and then woke up a bit. "What's the matter with *you*?" she asked Annabel, who was scarlet in the face by now. Unfortunately, she said it round the cereal spoon, and Annabel nearly exploded with laughter.

"Oh," Katie took the spoon out of her mouth and went slightly pink. "Is that what she's laughing at?" she asked Becky, who was giggling, but nowhere near in the same state as Annabel.

"Yup. Sorry, Katie, but you had the funniest look on your face, like your brain had totally gone on holiday. What on earth were you thinking about?"

"Football shirts. I was wondering if we could raise money to buy them ourselves. The team, I mean. As the school can't."

Becky nodded thoughtfully, and Annabel managed to stop giggling for long enough to say, "Good idea. If you raised lots you could have better ones than the boys, that'd be cool."

Mum laughed. "It *is* a good idea. You should talk to

Mrs Ross about it. You three need to get going by the way, or you'll never be there on time."

The triplets heaved themselves up from the breakfast table and went to find their stuff. Getting to school on Monday mornings was always more of a trudge than other days, somehow.

When they got to school, Katie brightened up. The triplets had met up with Saima and Fran on the way, and now she could see Megan waiting for them by the horse chestnut tree in the playground. Megan was sitting on one of the huge twisted roots that made the tree such a good place for meeting and chatting. She looked semi-comatose, and not particularly in a state to be enthusiastic about energetic fund-raising plans. But when Katie sat down next to her and said, "How would you like us to have our own proper team shirts?" she did manage an enquiring look.

"What? How?"

"We could raise the money for them ourselves. I bet we can. People are always raising money for things."

Katie waved a hand vaguely. She hadn't got much further than deciding to raise the money. She'd figure out *how* later! "Will you come with me and ask Mrs Ross at practice tonight?"

"Mmm." Megan nodded thoughtfully. "It's a good idea. We definitely need our own shirts. Your sister was right – we did look silly on Friday."

For Megan and Katie, that Monday seemed extra-long, and as soon as school finished they dashed off to the changing rooms to get into their sports kit and grab Mrs Ross.

The coach was pulling a big net of balls out of the PE storeroom, and she looked pleased to see them. "Hello, you two – wow, you moved fast, it's only twenty to four. And congratulations, by the way. I didn't have much time to talk to you on Friday, but you both played really well, especially as it was your first match."

Megan flushed as red as her hair with pleasure, and Katie was tongue-tied. Mrs Ross seemed to accept their beaming smiles as answer enough, though. She grinned back. "Did you want anything special? Or are you just feeling helpful?"

"Oh!" Katie had almost forgotten about their mission after Mrs Ross had been so nice. "Well, we did come to help. . ." she tailed off and smiled shyly.

"But. . .?" said Mrs Ross, with her head on one side like a curious bird.

"We had an idea we wanted to ask you about. It was my sister that made us think of it." Katie glanced at Megan, who was nodding in encouragement. "She asked why we didn't have a proper team strip like the Hillcrest side did."

"Annabel said she thought we didn't look as good as the Hillcrest team," chimed in Megan. "She thought we looked a bit silly, just in our PE kit."

Mrs Ross made a face. "I'm sorry, girls. I know it's annoying that you don't have a real strip – especially when you're doing so well. Team shirts cost a lot, that's the problem. I know a proper kit for you is one of the things on the PE department's list of stuff it wants to spend money on – but I'm afraid it's quite a long list."

"Oh, we know," Katie jumped in eagerly. "That's why we came up with this idea. We were wondering if *we* could raise the money. The team, I mean."

"Do you think we could, Mrs Ross?" Megan asked hopefully.

The coach looked thoughtful. "It's a big commitment. But I do think it's a very good idea. And it would show everyone that you girls *are* committed." Privately Mrs Ross was also thinking that it might be a good way to bond the team together a bit more. If Katie, Megan and Cara were going to stay on the team – and that would depend on how they played, and on Michelle, Lizzie and Caroline, whose places they'd taken – the Year Eights needed to get used to the idea. Maybe working together on something like this would help. She smiled. "I'll talk to everyone at the end of practice – now, can you two carry these balls out to the pitch?"

Football practice didn't leave much room for thinking about anything apart from what a slave-driver Mrs Ross was, so it wasn't until the end of the session when the exhausted team had put their sweaters back on and flopped down on the grass for Mrs Ross to talk to them, that Katie and Megan remembered what she was going to talk *about*.

"Well done, everybody. Lots of hard work going on there. And congratulations to all of you on last Friday's result. That was a really excellent game. You do realize, don't you, that if we keep this up we've got a really good chance of being in the league final? The semi-final's on Wednesday – yes, you did know that, Kiran, it was on the sheet we sent out at the beginning of term!" Mrs Ross glared at Kiran, who'd been looking blank at this announcement, but she was well known to be a bit scatty. Then Mrs Ross smiled again. "Now, I've got an interesting suggestion for all of you. I know that you'd all like to have your own team strip –" she paused to let the chorus of "ooh"s and "yes"s roll over her – "but the school's not been able to pay for one yet. Katie and Megan have suggested that we try to raise money for new shirts for all of you ourselves. What do you think? It would mean raising about three hundred pounds to pay to have a sufficient number of shirts made, I know it sounds a lot, but –" She paused again to see what sort of reaction the team was giving.

The team captain, Sarah, who was *very* popular, and quite scary, turned to Katie. "Your idea?" She sounded slightly surprised that a Year Seven could actually have ideas at all, let alone a good one. Katie fought down a snappy reply and just nodded – she had something of the same feeling about the team as Mrs Ross, that it would be nice if they could all get along. "What kind of stuff do you want to do to raise the money?"

Katie shrugged. "I don't know, I didn't really get that far. A cake sale, or something?"

"Sponsored laps round the field!" broke in someone else, and everyone groaned, but the fund-raising idea was definitely popular – people were chattering excitedly about what they could do.

"Why don't you all have a think before Wednesday's match?" Mrs Ross suggested, pleased with the way they were now all coming up with plans. "The team list will go up tomorrow morning, so remember to check. By the minibus at quarter to four, please, those of you who're playing! Off you go, then."

As they headed back to the changing rooms, Katie and Megan wondered about their chances of being in the team again.

"We were both OK on Friday," mused Megan. "Well,

you were more than OK, I mean, two goals, Mrs Ross would be mad to leave you out."

"Depends on those Year Eights, though, doesn't it? Michelle and Lizzie were back at practice today. Mrs Ross might give them another chance—" She broke off as Cara Peters caught up with them and walked alongside her. What on earth did she want? It was just *possible* that she wanted to talk about the fund-raising plan, she'd had an idea, maybe. But then again . . . this was Cara.

"Nice idea." Katie immediately felt guilty, but Cara carried on, "I suppose you've got sick of just bossing your sisters around."

"What?" Katie felt completely wrong-footed – she had no idea what Cara was talking about.

"A whole football team doing what Katie Ryan says. Now that's more like it. Got any more bright ideas? I suppose Mrs Ross has arranged for you to take over training as well?"

"Shut up, Cara, that's so stupid!" broke in Megan. "Anyway, you can't talk, you spend your whole life hanging on every word Amy Mannering says."

Cara flushed angrily, but ignored Megan and carried on taunting Katie. "Maybe Becky and Annabel got sick of it? Didn't want to do exactly what their darling sister said any more? Was that it – you needed a new set of slaves?"

Katie folded her arms and gave Cara a pitying stare. "Just because Amy treats you like dirt, you think everyone's the same. Get it through your thick skull – she's a bossy little madam and you're a mindless moron."

"I'll tell Amy you said that!" Cara spat out, as if it was the ultimate threat.

"Sorry, am I supposed to be scared? Grow up, Cara. It's nothing to do with being bossy, I just like being on a football team. The only thing I don't like is having to be on it with you, because you're – well, you're just a nuisance. Like a buzzy fly." And having reduced Cara to the status of an insect, Katie grabbed Megan's arm and they walked off to the changing rooms, leaving Cara still trying to think of a good answer.

Megan chuckled. "She's going to have to hang around outside until we've got changed now – she'll never dare come in, you might start again. She is *such* an idiot."

"Mmmm." Katie grinned briefly. Squashing Cara had been fun, but somehow, she didn't feel quite as triumphant as she usually did after dealing with someone who'd been mean to her. People did pick on the triplets sometimes – they were different, and they got a lot of attention, and some people couldn't cope with that. Normally it was water off a duck's back to Katie – Becky hated arguments, but Katie and Annabel could give as good as they got and enjoy it. So why was she feeling odd, and worried? She had to snap out of it – first that stupid thing with Megan and her dad on Friday, and now this! But although Cara Peters was a total idiot, Katie had a horrible feeling that for once, she might have managed to notice something important. . .

Chapter Four

Katie was remarkably silent all that evening. She ate her stir-fried chicken and noodles almost mechanically and failed to laugh at Annabel when she twirled so many noodles round her fork that she had a practically tennis-ball-sized mouthful to deal with. She did actually manage to get it in her mouth, but then she was stuck, looking like a hamster that had *seriously* overreached itself. Mum had been called away to the phone and Annabel had rather been expecting that Katie would shunt into her big-sister mode and forbid her to put it in her mouth, or try to, anyway. She'd been quite looking forward to telling Katie to mind her own business and stop behaving like her mother. But Katie just gazed at her, looking troubled, and definitely not-all-there.

Becky threw Annabel a worried glance, and Annabel finished choking down her super-sized noodle nightmare

39

and brandished the now-empty fork at her sister. "What's up?" she demanded, ignoring Becky's frowned signals, which were *supposed* to tell her not to make Katie more upset. "You look like Pixie when she's just missed a really juicy-looking pigeon."

"Nothing," muttered Katie edgily.

Becky and Annabel gave her sternly disbelieving looks, but Mum came back into the kitchen just then and they could sense that Katie wouldn't thank them for making whatever it was that was wrong obvious. Annabel gave her a "later" look and started to prattle distractingly to Mum about the boringness of the lessons they'd had that day.

After tea they watched a bit of TV, but Mum was still very much in evidence, so Annabel's plans had to be put on hold. Eventually Mum gave them a meaningful look and they sloped off to do their homework – Annabel to her personal study-space, otherwise known as halfway up the stairs, and Becky and Katie to the big desk in their bedroom. "Homework first, then we want the full story," hissed Annabel as they headed out of the living room. "Don't we, Becky?"

Becky grinned sympathetically at Katie. Annabel was *very* stubborn, and Katie clearly wasn't going to get away with not telling them what was going on.

Despite the fact that in theory she had homework to do for French, Maths and History, Annabel was upstairs less than an hour later, perched on the edge of the desk and demanding details.

"But I haven't finished!" wailed Katie, sounding truly upset.

Annabel was surprised – this was not normal Katie behaviour. Interrupting her homework (unless she was bored and wanted to be interrupted) would normally get you seriously snapped at, if not shoved off the edge of the desk (and Maths textbook) you happened to be sitting on. This was Katie in a tizz – very rare.

"Oh. Well, OK. Quarter of an hour?"

"'Kay," came a muffled answer, as Katie bent over her Maths again.

Annabel raised her eyebrows at Becky over Katie's head, and Becky responded with a wide-eyed look and the tiniest shrug – *no idea*. Annabel flounced out of the room to fetch her Maths books. If she had to wait for quarter of an hour, she might as well make use of the time to deal with the Maths exercise that she had not so much done, as, well, *looked* at. She slumped on her bed and proceeded to growl at her textbook.

Quarter of an hour and not very many trigonometry questions later, Annabel was back, though she'd taken note of Katie's emotional state earlier, and the "Be careful!" look that Becky was giving her, and was employing tact and gentleness – or so she thought.

"Katie. . . Have you finished yet? You have, haven't you? *I've* finished, so you must have done." Katie was very good at Maths, which had the unfair (according to Annabel) effect of making everyone think that Becky and Annabel were, too. People had an annoying tendency to do that sort of thing. There were lots of brilliant things about being triplets, but that was one of the downsides. It annoyed all of them, but particularly Katie, when people really did just assume they were the same in every way, rather than just looking the same. They were doing the best they could to make sure that everyone at Manor Hill knew they were Katie and Becky and Annabel, and not just "the triplets".

Katie shoved her books into her rucksack, and Becky did the same. She might have to do a bit of catching up tomorrow breaktime, but she could see that Katie needed help now – even if she didn't want it.

Katie went over to her bed and sat down cross-legged, then fossicked around down the side of the bed for the worn, faded and now rather dusty toy dog that she'd had as long as she could remember. Most of the time she wasn't a cuddly-toy person, hence Horse's frequent stays down the side of her bed, but occasionally she needed him. (Katie knew quite well that Horse was a dog, but she hadn't *at the time*, and she refused to change his name now.)

Becky and Annabel sat down on the end of her bed, facing her, and Annabel, still being "tactful", asked, "So what's up?"

Katie stared at what was left of Horse's ears. "Do I boss you around too much?" she asked quietly.

"Yup," said Annabel, grinning, but Becky poked her, and wriggled closer to Katie.

"Only in a good way – we'd spend half the time in the wrong classroom with the wrong books and the wrong people if you didn't get us organized. Look at Annabel messing up that French test when you two weren't talking before half-term. . . Why, Katie? I mean, why'd you suddenly ask that?"

"No reason," a small, very unconvincing voice replied.

"You're a really bad liar, Katie Ryan." Annabel grinned. "Another reason why we love you. Someone called you a bossy little know-all, didn't they? Who was it? Only I'm allowed to do that."

"I'm serious!" Katie sounded really upset, for her, and Annabel sobered up again.

"So am I. Who was it? They're going to be really sorry they were horrible to you."

"Tell us, Katie," Becky persuaded. "They must have said something really awful to make you feel like this, 'cause normally you couldn't care less what people say."

"I do if it's about you two as well," Katie pointed out miserably. "It was Cara."

"Oh well, there's a surprise," said Annabel sarcastically. "Why are you paying attention to anything that poisonous little rat says? She probably had to have Amy write it out on a bit of paper for her! Honestly, Katie, you *are* an idiot." Annabel said this very affectionately, and gave her sister a quick hug. Cara had been mean, Katie had stupidly taken it seriously – end of subject.

Becky wasn't so sure. Super-sensible Katie seemed really thrown, and come to think of it, she'd been a little bit funny all weekend, ever since the match on Friday. Something was definitely wrong. "What did Cara say about me and Annabel? *Exactly*." She fixed Katie with a firm glare.

Katie sighed. "She said that I was bossing everybody in the football team around – Megan and I told Mrs Ross about my idea to try and raise money for a real football strip, you see – and she said it was because you two had got tired of me bossing you all the time and I'd had to find somebody else." She sniffed.

"*Katie!*" Becky and Annabel sounded disgusted, partly with their sister, and mostly with Cara. Annabel added, "You are such a *twit*. If me and Becky thought you were bossing us about, we'd say so."

Becky nodded fiercely. "You don't anyway—"

"Much," giggled Annabel irrepressibly, and Becky smacked her round the back of the head, not hard at all, but it was enough to make Annabel howl with indignation, and rub her head as if she'd been knocked into the middle of next week.

"Shut *up*, Bel! Honestly, you just don't know when to stop." Becky put her arm round Katie, and scowled at Annabel until she came and sat on Katie's other side.

"You don't boss us around, Katie. You're just way more organized than we are. If we're about to be late, or go to the wrong classroom, or forget Mum's birthday, or *whatever*, you tell us. That's not bossing, that's *helping*. We let you do it too much, that's all."

Katie had been looking as though she desperately wanted to believe what Becky was telling her, but her face fell in the middle of Becky's little speech. *Too much?*

Becky rushed on desperately as she saw Katie's eyes widen and darken. "I just mean because me and Annabel

46

are lazy. One of these days you'll be sick or something, and we'll be in a state – we shouldn't let you do everything for us, that's all."

"Speak for yourself," yawned Annabel. "I like having Katie to organize me – she's good at it and I'm not, so why should I bother?"

"I'll thump you again," Becky warned. "This is important, Bel!"

"I just don't get why you're both taking this so seriously. Cara's a prat, we don't care what she thinks, why *go on* about it?"

Becky caught her eye meaningfully, and Annabel looked harder at Katie holding her old toy dog, suddenly realizing just how out of character her sister was behaving. "Unless there's something else wrong as well, Katie? Is that why you can't just snap out of it?"

Katie went back to her examination of Horse's ears.

"There is, isn't there? I knew it!" said Annabel triumphantly. "You were a bit quiet all weekend, but I thought you were just grumpy after what I said about you looking silly without proper football clothes."

"I got really cross with Megan on Friday," admitted Katie, unhappily.

"With *Megan*?" Becky sounded shocked.

"You did not, Katie Ryan, or if you did it was the fastest fight and make-up in history," accused Annabel. "We didn't notice a thing, and we would've done – we were all sleeping in here!"

"I didn't *tell* her I was cross," Katie explained. "It wasn't her fault at all. I was jealous."

Becky shook her head. "How could you be jealous of Megan? You played way better than she did—"

"I know!" snarled Katie, remembering the unfairness of it all over again. "I was jealous 'cause she had her dad there, and he was so excited for her, and really proud of her – did you see him, leaping up and down like a mad thing? She didn't even do anything that special and he was acting like she – she. . ." Katie trailed off and stared at Horse's ears miserably, and Becky and Annabel, who'd relaxed their comfort-hug while they tried to work out what was going on, went back into support mode immediately.

Unfortunately, though, hugging was about all they

could manage. What could they say? Katie was right –
it wasn't fair, but there was no way they could
magically make it all better. Their dad was always going
to be working abroad, as far as they could see.

"Dad's coming back at Christmas," Becky ventured.
"Maybe he'll see you play then."

"I suppose," agreed Katie sadly. "It was such a cool
game on Friday, though. And then that night I was
thinking about how he used to play football with me in
the garden. We did that a bit when he came back at half-
term, but it wasn't the same – it used to be every
weekend. And if it was raining we'd watch the football on
TV instead. I just really, really hate him not being here."

"Me too," murmured Becky, and Annabel sighed.

But Katie couldn't help thinking that her sisters
didn't really understand. Because she was the sporty
one of the triplets and her dad was really into sport too,
they'd always been close. Becky and Annabel missed
him, of course they did – but Katie just couldn't believe
it was the same for them.

Chapter Five

On the way up to the school gates next morning, the triplets were shambling sleepily along when a whirlwind suddenly attacked Katie. It was Megan, flailing bags and bubbling over with excitement.

"What's the matter with you?" Annabel asked grumpily. She'd nearly slipped off the kerb when Megan threw herself at Katie.

"Football match!" squeaked Megan, who'd run after the triplets halfway up the road and was now completely out of breath.

"No, it's on Wednesday – today's Tuesday," replied Katie in surprise – Megan was usually very organized, especially about football. "Oh, you mean we've got to go and check the team list?"

"No, no, no!" Megan was recovering the power of speech now, and started to explain properly. "I mean, yes we have, and I reckon we can dash and look on the board before registration if we're super-fast, but I've had an idea for raising money. I think we should set up a special football match and make people pay for tickets."

"Yeah, 'cause everyone's going to pay loads of money to see you lot prancing around a field," snarled Annabel, who really wasn't a morning person, "Can we pay *not* to have a ticket?"

Megan gave her a "ha ha, very funny" kind of look. "I haven't finished, Little Miss Grumpy. The special thing about this match is who we play. . ." She paused, gathering everyone's attention, her eyes sparkling and her ginger curls positively twitching with excitement.

"Go on then," urged Katie, her interest caught now.

"The boys' team!" Megan said, delighted with her own cleverness. "Oh, come on, we'd slaughter them, it would be absolutely fantastic!"

"Yeees," agreed Katie thoughtfully, her eyes lighting up as she considered the idea. "And I bet people would want to buy tickets; all the girls *ought* to want to cheer us on, and the boys will be convinced we're rubbish

51

and want to see us get really shown up. I think it's an ace plan, Megan! Did it just come to you?"

"Woke up in the middle of the night with it," nodded Megan happily. "It's how I always have my best ideas, but normally I don't really remember them in the morning, or I just have half the idea, you know? Like I know it was something about aardvarks. So I actually got up *in the middle of the night* and wrote it on the bathroom mirror in lipgloss 'cause I couldn't find any paper. My mum was furious, and she just wouldn't understand even when I tried to explain how important it was. So now I have to clean the bathroom at the weekend."

"I suppose it would be fun to see those boys lose really badly," mused Annabel. "Especially if you managed to injure Max somehow. So are you going to sell tickets? When do you think it'll be?"

"Slow down!" Megan laughed. "We need to get permission from – well, I don't know who – everybody, I should think."

"And we'd have to check that the rest of the team are up for it – I can't see why they wouldn't be, but you never know," added Katie.

"Yeah, Year Eights." Megan shrugged. They were all a bit weird and unpredictable. "I reckon we ought to go and talk to them about it, before we ask Mrs Ross?" She raised her eyebrows hopefully at Katie.

"You're right. We'd better go and find them all at break." Katie made a face – it wasn't exactly a fun prospect, as the Year Eights were bound to be a bit sniffy. It wasn't as if they were that much older even – only a year – but they seemed to think it made them special. Suddenly Katie had a horrible thought. Was this the kind of bossiness that Cara had accused her of? Wanting to take over everything? But that was stupid – she just wanted to get things *done*. She banished Cara to the back of her mind again, and said firmly, "Maybe we'd better find Sarah first. She's the captain, and she seemed to think us raising money was a good idea. If we can get her on our side, maybe the others'll agree too."

It was decided – Megan and Katie were off on a mission at break. Just then the bell went, and Megan and Katie gave each other half-scared, half-excited looks and made a run for the PE department's noticeboard by the staffroom, while all the others headed off to the classroom, promising to cover for them if Miss Fraser was early. Katie pelted up to the noticeboard. She was still feeling slightly miserable deep down, but she was building up a hard shell to cover it, one that she wouldn't let even her sisters or her best friend break. However, seeing her name high up on the list for Wednesday's game chased the niggling feeling out of her completely. Until she turned round, grinning, and looked at Megan, who was *not* grinning. Katie whipped back to the board – Megan was down as a sub, but Michelle, one of the Year Eight girls who'd missed practices, was back in goal.

"Oh, Megan, that's so unfair! You're way better than Michelle!" Katie gave Megan a quick hug, and felt guilty – she'd been so pleased to see her name that she'd totally forgotten her friend.

Megan smiled, with an effort. "At least I'm a sub, I suppose that's better than nothing. Well done."

Then they caught sight of the clock, gasped, and ran for it.

Meanwhile, Becky and Annabel were using the time without their sister to ask for advice. Katie was being Katie – determined, super-committed to her football and a complete muppet (the last bit was a quote from Annabel). She was obviously missing their dad like anything, and they were sure that her overreaction to Cara was all mixed up with that too. Of course Katie was bossy! It wasn't because there was anything wrong with her, she was just a very sensible person who had good ideas and liked organizing people. But now Katie seemed to have lost some of her bounce, and she was refusing to talk about it, which was worse. It was as though she felt she'd been un-Katie-ish enough with their heart-to-heart the night before. There had to be something Annabel and Becky could do to make her feel better, but they just couldn't work out what it was. So they huddled round their table with Saima and Fran, and started to explain. They were looking very shifty, because they knew Katie would kill them if she found out they'd been talking about her.

"Look," murmured Annabel, flicking a suspicious glance round the classroom, and sticking her tongue out at Max Cooper, who happened to catch her eye, "we need some help. Katie's really missing our dad, 'cause he's not there to watch her play football, and we need some ideas on how to cheer her up."

"And it's got to be a secret," added Becky hurriedly, carefully pretending not to see Max, who was now glaring in their direction, and casting an anxious look at Amy and Cara and Emily, who were admiring Amy's nails. She really didn't want *them* to hear all about Katie's problems. "Katie would be embarrassed we told you, you know what she's like."

Saima steepled her fingers and looked thoughtful. "Could you talk to your dad about it? I mean, do you think he knows how she feels?"

Becky and Annabel looked blankly at each other. *Did* Dad know? E-mail and the occasional phone call were all very well, but Dad being thousands of kilometres away meant no more of those useful moments where you just happened to mention that you could really do with new ballet shoes, or your sister was feeling down.

"I don't think she'd have said anything," pondered

Becky. "I mean, she e-mails him a lot, but she likes him to think she's doing OK. You know – that she's really sorted."

"Perfect," snorted Annabel. "That's what Katie always has to be."

"But do you think *we* should tell him?" Becky looked anxious. "We might make them *both* upset."

Saima shrugged. "But don't you think he'd want to know?" she asked.

Annabel and Becky exchanged glances – they'd have to think about this. "Hmm," said Becky after a moment. "Maybe we *should* e-mail Dad."

"Joy," said Annabel gloomily. "*That*'ll be a fun e-mail to write."

Just then Miss Fraser came in with the register (and Becky suddenly realized that it was all very well answering for Katie, providing Miss Fraser was a bit sleepy, but how were they supposed to be red-haired Megan?). Luckily Katie and Megan skidded in behind her, looking solemn and out of breath.

"Are you in?" hissed Annabel, as they slipped into their places.

"Tell you later," murmured Katie, not wanting to make Megan feel any worse.

But Megan said quickly, "I'm only a sub this time. But Katie's up front again, with Sarah, and everybody's favourite little footballer." She jerked her head in Cara's direction, and then Miss Fraser started to call the register, and Megan was able to smile and pretend everything was OK.

Morning lessons seemed to race past for Katie – her brain really wasn't in school, it was out on the football field scoring spectacular goals while Cara Peters sulked on the subs bench, Max Cooper tripped over his own feet as Katie flew past him, and her dad told everyone on the sidelines that she was his daughter and she was going to play for Man United or maybe Barcelona – Katie's favourite European team. . .

When the bell went for break Katie and Megan headed for the far side of the playground where there was a grassy patch with a couple of benches. Year Tens and above were allowed to stay in at break and lunch if they wanted, so unless it was really sunny (in which case the whole school was fighting for a patch of grass so they could stretch out and sunbathe) the benches were Year Eight and Nine territory. Normally Year Nines got the benches and the Year Eights sat on jumpers or jackets or textbooks. Whatever, it *definitely* wasn't somewhere that two measly Year Sevens should be approaching. No one was going to bother themselves to *say* anything, of course, as Year Sevens were invisible, but the atmosphere was below freezing as Megan and Katie approached Sarah's little group. They'd been lucky to spot them early on in their search.

The older girls were deep in discussion, and Sarah hadn't noticed them, so Megan and Katie hung around the edge of the little group, getting a few curious glances, until Katie gave up waiting for Sarah to stop talking about *EastEnders*, and tapped her on the shoulder.

Sarah did not look particularly pleased to see them. "Er, yes?" she said, with a slight edge of frost on her voice.

Katie grinned at her team captain – Cara might have thrown her off balance yesterday, but frosty-voiced Year Eights weren't at all scary. Although Megan was standing behind Katie and pretending none of this had been her idea.

"Megan's had a brilliant idea about raising money for the team strip!" Katie hooked an arm behind her and dragged her friend forward.

Sarah looked interested – Katie and Megan might only be Year Sevens, but they had played well on Friday, and the new strip idea was something that Sarah wished she'd thought of.

"We thought maybe we could set up a special match – make people pay for tickets," said Megan nervously and shut up again.

She'd obviously gone as far as she was going, so Katie carried on, "But the cool thing is it'd be against the junior boys' team. Don't you think we could beat them?" she appealed to Sarah.

Sarah sat bolt upright and breathed an ecstatic, "Yes!" Then she actually jumped up. "Hey, of course we could. They're useless. That would be so fun. We should go and tell the others. Look, see you later, you lot, I'll be back in a bit."

Megan and Katie looked at each other in relief. This was even better than they'd hoped. Sarah actually put a hand on Megan's shoulder and propelled her over to the other end of the grass where several of the team were lounging and poring over the latest *J-17*. Sarah bounced up to them with Katie and Megan in tow and asked, with a gleam of mischief in her eyes, "How would you like to make the boys' junior team look like total muppets in front of the whole school?"

That got everyone's attention. "We play them to raise money for our shirts. *She* thought of it – " Sarah indicated Megan in a way that suggested independent thought and Year Sevens didn't usually go together – "but it's a brilliant idea. After all the stuff they've said about us, we'll really show them."

There was general enthusiasm, and as they'd now got at least half the team to agree, Sarah, Megan and Katie reckoned the plan was pretty much on. Katie suggested that she and Megan ask Mrs Ross about it in their PE lesson on Wednesday morning and Sarah was all for it. She rushed off to see if she could find any more of the team, and promised she'd sound them all out before Wednesday's match, but she was certain they'd want to do it. As she disappeared, she threw back over her shoulder, "Can you find that other girl in your class, what's-her-name? Tell her too!"

Katie and Megan exchanged dismayed glances, then sighed and set off to find Cara. As it turned out, by the time they got to her – with Amy and Emily as usual – she already knew. Sarah had been working fast, and the gossip was already spreading. Amy went into attack mode as soon as she saw Katie approaching.

"Oh, *look*. Now which one's this? Very scruffy, so not Annabel. And accompanied by a walking carrot. Hello Katie, hello whatever-your-name-is!" Amy smiled a charmingly nasty smile.

"Oh, shut up," snapped Katie disgustedly; she hadn't time for swapping insults with the self-proclaimed queen of Year Seven, and talking to Cara again after her worrying comments on Monday was making her feel tetchy. "Cara, we're all going to play a fund-raising match against the boys, OK? We're going to ask Mrs Ross about it in PE tomorrow, you can come if you like."

Cara sneered – she'd obviously recovered from their spat the afternoon before, or perhaps it was having Amy and Emily to back her up. "Oh, *thank* you, Katie. Can I lick your boots now? I can't believe how conceited you are. I get to come with you to ask Mrs Ross about your little plan? Wow, what an honour. I think I might die of excitement."

"Don't, then," said Katie. "We were only trying to be nice, so you didn't feel left out. We won't bother next time."

"Whose stupid idea was this anyway? Yours?"

"No, it was Megan's, and it's not stupid – everyone else likes it," snapped Katie. "What's wrong with it?"

Cara hadn't thought this far. "It's just stupid," she replied lamely. "Obviously."

"So you don't reckon we can win?" put in Megan.

"No, of course it's not that," blustered Cara, looking to Amy and Emily for help and not getting any.

"She's scared," sneered Megan to Katie, and they both giggled.

"I am not!"

"So you'll be up for it, then?" demanded Katie.

Cara sighed, as though she couldn't believe she was being forced to join in something so childish. "I suppose so. If we have to. But don't think it's because I want to, Katie Ryan. Only because you'll get slaughtered if I don't play." She smirked, and Katie and Megan exchanged disgusted glances and walked away. Really, there was no point even bothering to be nice to people like that. But still! The plan was going ahead, and Manor Hill Junior Boys were about to get the shock of their lives!

Becky and Annabel spent the rest of the day giving each other worried, thoughtful looks. Even Annabel's bouncy, happy-go-lucky personality was a little bit dampened. Luckily, Katie was so preoccupied that she didn't notice, but Saima felt quite guilty, and whispered to Fran in Science that she wished she'd never suggested they talk to their dad about it.

When the triplets got home that night, Katie was full

of the fund-raising plan, and so determinedly enthusiastic about the match against the boys that Annabel and Becky had to look at her carefully as she chattered to Mum over tea. Was this really someone who was miserable, even deep down? But there was something about the intense brightness of Katie's voice that didn't ring true, and when she went off to do a bit of quick practising in the garden they nipped into the living room to work out what they were going to do under cover of watching TV.

"Do you really think we should tell Dad about Katie?" asked Becky anxiously. "I mean, it's not as if there's anything he can do about it either."

Annabel put her thumbnail in her mouth thoughtfully, then took it out when she remembered that she never, ever chewed her nails. "Mmm. Maybe we could tell him, but not in an 'it's all your fault' kind of way. Get him to do something to help – can't think what though."

"It needs to be something that shows Katie that he misses playing football with her too, I think. I mean, that would make her feel better. And maybe if he admits it, she might be able to think about it more."

"Without deciding that she's being silly and babyish and she isn't allowed to do anything as soppy as miss people, which I reckon is what she's doing now," added Annabel, in a moment of insight. "Let's go and e-mail Dad before Katie comes in. Come on!"

They dashed upstairs and logged on, Annabel using her separate e-mail address rather than their joint one.

```
From:Superstar.3ryans@mailserve.com
To: dryan@fostermarcus.co.uk
Subject: Katie
```

```
Hi Dad,
Have you noticed Katie being a bit
funny in e-mails recently? Becky
and I think she's really missing
you being here to do sporty-type
stuff with her like you used to.
```

Here Annabel stopped. "Now what? What are we actually supposed to *do* about it?"

Becky considered. "Weeeell, I was wondering if we

could do some kind of scrapbook thing that we could send Dad. I mean, we've got the camera – we could make a photo-diary of Katie, so that she feels like Dad's really seeing everything."

"Yes! And we can e-mail it all to him, so it's like a daily update. That's a brilliant idea!" And Annabel hugged her sister, nearly knocking her off the chair they were sharing, before starting to type furiously again.

```
We're going to start sending you
lots of photos of Katie doing
football stuff (she's doing loads
of training). I'm going to take the
photos, and Becky'll do captions
for them, and write stuff.
```

"Hey! When did we decide that? I might want to take the photos, it was my idea!" squeaked Becky indignantly.

Annabel gazed at her, blue eyes very wide and innocent. "But Becky, you're so *good* at that sort of thing. Loads better than me – you know you are."

Becky glared back at her sister, looking like a ruffled

kitten. "You are such a liar, Annabel. You got an A for your last English essay, and Mr Marshall said it was brilliantly imaginative – you showed everybody."

"It was a fluke," said Annabel airily. "It was about what you wanted to be when you grow up, and it wasn't imaginative, it's all going to happen."

"Oh, all right, when you're making millions in Hollywood you'd just better remember this," grumbled Becky, giving in as usual – somehow Annabel was good at getting people to do *exactly* what she wanted.

Annabel went back to typing:

```
We think this might cheer Katie
up - when we tell her that you've
been watching her every move! What
do you think?
Lots of love,
Bel and Becky
```

Then they shut down the computer, and grinned at each other – Operation Cheer-Up-Katie was on!

Chapter Six

Year Seven had PE first thing on Wednesday mornings. Apart from the sports-mad people like Katie, it wasn't very popular.

As Saima said that particular morning, "It's just cruel to make us run around a field before we've even woken up. We need something nice and gentle to get us going, like Geography."

Everyone else gave her slightly odd looks – Geography was so gentle it was practically coma-inducing, it was possibly *the* most boring subject ever invented. Who *cared* why volcanoes exploded? They didn't even get any decent videos.

"Just lurk at the back, Saima," advised Annabel, yawning.

By contrast, Megan and Katie were positively leaping

up and down with excitement, Katie especially, as there were things she was trying to put out of her head, and being excited about the fund-raising match helped. They were desperate to find Mrs Ross and get an official go-ahead for their big plans, And for some reason they expected the same amount of enthusiasm from everybody else. . .

"What is *with* you lot this morning?" Katie asked disgustedly, as she rocked herself from heel to toe to get her calf muscles warmed up. "You look like you don't even want to be here!"

Becky, Annabel, Saima and Fran exchanged long-suffering glances.

"Just be grateful," said Annabel gloomily. "Becky and I get this *all the time*. Katie, please get it through your thick skull – we *don't* want to be here. We'd rather be anywhere else than here. In fact, here is the last place on Earth I want to be!"

Annabel had been taking Katie's horrified expression as a sign that her "we hate PE, or at any rate we do in the early morning" message was getting through. Unfortunately, though, it was actually a "shut up, shut up, shut up for heaven's sake, Mrs Ross is right behind you" expression.

"Goodness *me*, Annabel," said the PE teacher gently. "You really don't want to be here." She smiled. "Well, how about the other side of the field? Why don't you run over there, and then come back and let me know if it's any better on that side?"

Annabel looked at Mrs Ross blankly. She was feeling slightly shell-shocked.

"That wasn't a suggestion, Annabel. Now, please."

Annabel sighed and set off – really, it was so unfair the way teachers did that creeping up on you thing. Everyone else attempted to look as though they were actually just cunningly disguised blades of grass, in the hope that Mrs Ross would just ignore them. Except of course for Megan and Katie, who were delighted to have her attention.

"Mrs Ross, Mrs Ross," squeaked Katie in excitement, "Megan's had the best idea, can we just tell you about it really quickly? Oh, and sorry about Annabel," Katie added quickly, catching sight of her sister jogging across the field at mouse-speed and clutching her side in an obvious attempt to show everybody that she was dying of the worst stitch anybody had ever had. "She didn't mean it, honestly."

"Hmmm," was all Mrs Ross managed, but at least it wasn't a "shut up and go away" kind of hmmm, so Katie took it as encouragement, and pushed Megan forward.

"Please, Mrs Ross, can we arrange a kind of charity football match, between us and the boys' team? Everyone pays for tickets, and we get to show them how good we are!" enthused Megan.

Mrs Ross brightened up. "What a good idea!"

"We checked with the rest of the team," Katie reassured her (this was true, Sarah had given her a massive thumbs-up in assembly that morning, so she reckoned that they had the whole squad on side). "Everyone wants to. Do you think the boys will go for it?"

Mrs Ross grinned, looking at the boys, who were over the other side of the field with a different teacher. Only three of the boys' team were in the triplets' Year Seven class: Max (the triplets' personal worst enemy), his mate Ben, and David, a boy who'd only moved to Darefield quite recently. David was actually really nice, and the triplets had invited him to their birthday party a few weeks earlier, because Becky thought he needed a bit of looking after. Now, though, he was looking quite chummy with Max, and the pair of them were shooting dagger-looks at Katie.

"I think Mr Anderson might have trouble holding them back," Mrs Ross said, nodding in Max and David's direction. "Looks like the news is spreading fast. I'll talk to the rest of the PE staff about your idea."

Annabel came puffing back from her trip across the field, an agonized, martyred expression on her face. Mrs Ross gave her a beaming smile, and sent the entire class off to run all the way round the field. "Don't look like that, Annabel – you must be nicely warmed up by now."

At morning break, Katie and Megan found out with a vengeance that Mrs Ross was right. The boys *did* know about the match, and they were furious.

David was too nice to do anything apart from grin hugely and tell them, "Watch out, you two – we're going to win by probably about a million goals."

But Max didn't hold back. He swaggered up to the chestnut tree where the triplets and their friends were sharing Fran's crisps, and posed arrogantly in front of them.

"What do *you* want?" sighed Katie, as contemptuously as possible.

Max smirked. "Just to let you know that you're dead. Your stupid girly lot won't know what's hit them when they play a proper team. You're gonna lose big-time."

"We're in the league semi-finals, you know," Megan put in. "'Scuse me for mentioning it, but didn't your team get knocked out in the quarter-final last week? I seem to remember you lost three–nil."

Max shuffled his feet. "Yeah, well, we were playing decent teams, not *girls*. You're only in the semis because the rest of the girls' teams are even more useless than you. Just wait." He waved a finger at them threateningly and turned on his heel, leaving the girls collapsing with giggles.

"Oooh, Katie," chirped Annabel. "You're *dead*! Aren't you scared? Big bad Maxie's gonna get you!"

Max's ears turned scarlet as he headed back to his mates – somehow the girls hadn't seemed suitably scared. He hadn't expected they'd admit to it, but he'd thought they might have got cross, not just think it was funny! He really, really hated Katie Ryan. Perfect hair, perfect face, nasty little perfect smile. . . Well, he'd show them. The girls were going to get slaughtered – then see who was laughing.

At quarter to four that afternoon, the girls' team were gathering by the minibus in the school car park. Everyone was excited – not only were they about to play in the semi-final, but the gossip about their possible fund-raising match had spread round the whole school, and everyone was buzzing with it. It seemed as though it wasn't just Katie and Megan who'd had encounters with the opposition. Sarah was full of the shouting match she'd had with a couple of Year Eight boys who apparently thought that football was not for girls, ever, under any circumstances – but they were very kindly going to make an exception for this lot in order to show them exactly how useless they were.

"Go back to knitting! That's what they said!" Sarah was helpless with laughter. "Can you believe it? I just told them I wasn't their granny. What is it about football that turns some boys into total and utter morons? Seriously, though –" and Sarah looked round at everybody with a suitably serious expression on her face – "if this match does go ahead, we have absolutely *got* to win. We'll never live it down otherwise. We might have to do some extra training."

Everyone nodded firmly. Definitely. They had thought of the match as a fun thing up till now, but the boys seemed so furious that they'd even dared consider the idea, and had been such "macho posers" (Sarah's words) over the whole thing, that it was now deadly serious.

It felt really good being part of a team, and all being so keen on something. Even Cara had dropped her "it's stupid" attitude, and was looking as determined as everybody else. Katie looked round at everybody, grinning, and then looked again. Where was Michelle? Surely she couldn't have not bothered to turn up – a practice was one thing, but not to turn up to a *match*?

She nudged Megan, and whispered, "Michelle's not here!"

"I know!" Megan hissed back. "Do you think she's just late? The others haven't said anything. Shall we ask Sarah?"

Katie nodded vigorously, and then when Megan gave her a pleading look, sighed and turned to the team captain. "Sarah?"

"Yeah?"

"Where's Michelle? I mean, isn't she meant to be playing?"

"Oh! Megan, I'm really sorry, I was supposed to tell you! Michelle's gone home sick, so you have to be goalie. I was thinking about those stupid boys and I forgot. Lizzie's coming as sub." Sarah pointed to Lizzie, who was looking a bit sulky – being dropped in favour of Year Sevens, even when you had missed a few practices, wasn't exactly flattering.

Megan flushed scarlet (it clashed with her hair) with pleasure, and Katie hugged her.

"Excellent! That's so cool, you're much better in goal than Michelle. And if you play well in this match too, I reckon Mrs Ross will keep you in goal." She frowned. "Or maybe she'll keep alternating us all round, me and Cara and you and Michelle and the others." Then suddenly she pointed across the car park. "Look! Mrs Ross is coming. I wonder if she's spoken to Mr Anderson yet!"

The entire team, even Lizzie, surged across the car park to engulf their coach, but Mrs Ross refused to tell them anything until they were all on the minibus. "It's a good way to St Helen's," she pointed out. "You're going to need warm-up time, so let's get moving."

Everyone was so focused on getting info out of Mrs Ross that there wasn't even the usual squabble for the seats at the back, they just piled in and sat there with their ears pricked up, like dogs waiting for a bone.

At last they were on their way, and Mrs Ross finally agreed to part with her news. "But no shouting out questions, girls – I'm trying to drive here as well. OK.

Mr Anderson thinks it's a great idea—" Here she was cut off by a wave of cheering and waited, grinning to herself. When everyone had calmed down a bit, she added, "And that's not the best bit – Mr Anderson also said that it's definitely not fair that you don't have a team strip, so he reckons that any money you raise, the PE department will match out of its budget. So I reckon your shirts are pretty much guaranteed." This time the cheering was even louder, and Mrs Ross had to wait a couple of minutes before continuing. "So, we think that next Friday will be the best day, after school. We might be able to get afternoon lessons shortened if we talk nicely to Mr Brownfield. You think you'll be ready by then, girls?"

This was a serious question. Could they be ready?

"We definitely need to do some extra practice," Sarah told Mrs Ross. "Is it OK if we organize a session ourselves this weekend? In the park, maybe?"

"As long as you don't wear yourselves out. OK, we're here." Mrs Ross pulled into the gates of St Helen's School for Girls, a rather smart school that had a really strict uniform – perfect grey pleated skirts, red and gold ties, and red blazers. Apparently St Helen's girls were only allowed to wear red hairbands, the staff were that fussy. Their football kit was equally smart, though a bit of an eyeful – completely red, even the socks. *And* they had smart red fleeces with the school crest on to wear while they were warming up. The Manor Hill girls caught a few amused glances at their polo shirts, and felt even more determined – football shirts were a must!

But despite their perfect turn-out, St Helen's couldn't hold out against Manor Hill. The team had been getting better recently – it was as though everyone was actually working towards the same thing, rather than trying to look good and score on their own. At half-time the score was one–nil – Cara and Sarah had set up a brilliant goal between them, and Cara had actually headed it in, looking rather surprised that she managed it. Everyone who was anywhere near had hugged her, even Katie. Admittedly so many people had been trying to hug Cara that Katie hadn't actually touched her at all, but she still felt very virtuous about it.

The second half was harder. St Helen's had obviously been given a serious talking-to by somebody during the break, and they came back on to the field very determined. They still couldn't seem to score, but they were making a huge effort. Every time one of the Manor Hill forwards did anything it seemed as though a stubborn scarlet person popped up in front of them, and buzzed round them irritatingly like a really determined wasp. Luckily, though, Sarah and Cara had been getting most of the action in the first half, so the defence weren't paying quite as much attention to Katie.

Sarah was bright enough to spot this, and next time she passed Katie, she hissed in a not-too-obvious way, "Your turn!"

Katie nodded, and Sarah and Cara started to do some very fancy "we're-so-going-for-goals-look-at-us" stuff, which got the wasps practically hyperventilating in their eagerness to shut them down. And left Katie unmarked, and raring to go. There wasn't much time, though, just ten minutes left, and she was pretty sure that there was only one real chance for this – once she made a clear shot at goal the St Helen's girls would see that they had three dangerous players to concentrate on, not just two.

While Katie was worrying about all this, the perfect chance suddenly came up – and it worked! Sarah slipped her the ball, Cara faked a run at it that distracted the defenders and Katie whooshed up the field with it. The St Helen's goalkeeper was panicked. Nothing had got through the mad-keen defence for a while and she wasn't ready, now Katie was storming towards her – which way was the ball coming? She didn't seem to have Megan's telepathic abilities and dived to the wrong side of the net.

After that the St Helen's side went a bit sulky, and spent the last five minutes of the match not really trying. But the Manor Hill girls were jubilant – they were in the final!

Chapter Seven

At school on Thursday morning, everyone in the girls'
junior team was wandering about looking like cats that
had got the cream. Although, as Becky whispered
quietly to Fran as they perched on the chestnut tree in
the playground (Becky and Bel had managed to explain
their worries about Katie and the whole Dad situation
to Megan as well, though they'd carefully not
mentioned that it was *her* dad that had set the whole
thing off), Katie seemed to be alternating between
cream-stuffed cat and cat that had just fallen in the
pond while trying to catch the goldfish. . .

At registration, the triplets' table was positively
glowing with pride, and it didn't go unnoticed. David
came up to them to get the details on the match, and
Megan and Katie tried to look fairly modest about the
whole thing, but didn't manage all that well. As Megan

had pointed out to Max the other day, the boys' team had lost their league quarter-final match, and now the Manor Hill girls were in the final. It was hard not to gloat a bit, but they tried not to because David was nice.

"Well done." He grinned at Megan and Katie. "How did you manage that then, did they have their feet tied together?"

Katie grinned back. "Ha ha – jealous are we?"

He made a face. "Yeah, a bit – even if you don't win, it'll be really cool to be in the final. You'll all get those medals."

"You'll probably get in the final next year," put in Becky generously, smiling at David, which made him blush, and mutter something along the lines of "maybe". He was still grinning in a tongue-tied way when someone came up behind him.

"Hey, David! What are you talking to that lot for? Watch it, you might catch something."

It was Max, of course, and the triplets and the other girls groaned. Katie beamed at him. "Yeah, why don't you hang around too, Max? You never know, you might catch our winning streak – you sad loser."

Max took a step forward looking furious, and Katie stood up, so they were right in each other's faces. Max was practically spitting. "I told you before, you play in a stupid girls' league, and you are *nothing* – we're going to slaughter you next week, and the whole school is going to be watching."

"Yeah, watching us run circles round you, *Maxie*."

Becky and Annabel had stood up too by now – Katie was in the thick of an argument, and she was enjoying teasing Max, but she hadn't realized quite how angry he was getting. It really looked as if he would totally lose his temper if the argument carried on much longer, and they were worried.

David put a hand on Max's shoulder, and jerked his head at Max's mate Ben, who'd been watching and smirking a bit. "Leave it, Max. Come on, Miss Fraser'll be here in a minute, you'll get in trouble."

"Yeah, come on, Max. It's not worth it, mate," added Ben, and together they steered him away, still glaring at Katie, who was watching him go with a pitying smile on her face.

"Katie!" said Becky crossly. "You shouldn't do that,

you know what Max is like! One of these days you'll make him really mad at you, and then who knows what he might do!"

Katie sat down and tossed her ponytail irritatingly. "Oh, don't be a wuss, Becky. He wouldn't dare do anything." She looked round at the others, who were all giving her "Yeah, right!" looks, and frowned. "Oh, come on! He's an idiot, that's all, he's not even worth thinking about." And she smiled sunnily at them, and went back to checking she'd got all her books.

☆　❀　♡

After the semi-final, the girls' team had spent the minibus-trip home celebrating, and making plans for the fund-raising match. Katie had happily volunteered Annabel (and her and Becky *and* all their friends) to make posters and tickets. Annabel was brilliant at art, and so was Fran, so it seemed like the obvious answer – as Katie'd explained to a secretly flattered but pretend-annoyed Annabel that night. Everyone else in the team seemed happy to let them get on with it – it was loads of work! Katie really hadn't wanted the other major job that had to be done – luckily, Sarah, as captain, had been "volunteered".

In assembly on Friday morning Mr Brownfield, the head, had gone through all the usual boring stuff about litter, and the Manor Hill uniform being a badge that people recognized and how this somehow meant you had to behave well in the chip shop, and, as usual, everyone dozed with their eyes just open enough not to get told off. On their first day at Manor Hill the triplets had been really panicked by assembly – there were so many rules at this new school! Now they were much more relaxed.

Then, suddenly Mr Brownfield got interesting. "Now, I have a special announcement." He beamed round at everybody, and most people opened one eye to check whether this was an exciting new litter initiative, or something really interesting, "Could Sarah Barker from Year Eight come up on stage, please?"

Katie and Megan were bouncing with excitement – the match was official! Mr Brownfield got Sarah to explain what they were raising money for (*and* she told the whole school it was Katie's idea to get their new strip!) and then he announced that the match would be next Friday after school, and the teams would get out of last lesson to have time to warm up. It was excellent, and Mr Brownfield plugged the final as well, and said he was sure everyone would agree that such a successful team deserved a proper kit. Katie looked round and saw that the boys' team were looking green. There was a noticeable lack of admiring announcements about *them* in assembly at the moment. Katie, nudging Megan to point out the positively demonic expression on Max's face, felt a nervous shiver wriggle down her spine. *Obviously* she wasn't scared (of that lot?!) but she had a feeling that the boys were going to be doing whatever it took to win. . .

The triplets' bedroom was very full of people and bits of paper that evening, as Katie had rounded everybody up for a poster-making session. She and Megan were trying to work out exactly what the tickets should say on them before they went and printed them off on the computer, while the other four decorated huge sheets of paper for posters. It was annoying, Annabel pointed out, that because they were organizing the match they couldn't put what they really felt on the posters, like "Come and watch the fab girls' team show everyone what a load of two-left-footed eejits those boys are". Katie pointed out that they did want some boys to come and watch the match as well, though.

"In fact, as long as they pay for a ticket I don't care who comes. Does Feathers want to come, Fran?"

Feathers was Fran's gorgeous Golden Retriever. Fran giggled. "He'd love it, but he'd want to join in, and he's so dopey I wouldn't swear to it that he'd be playing for your lot. But you're practising in the park tomorrow, aren't you? I'll come and watch you, and I'll bring him then."

"Cool." Katie nodded. "Tomorrow afternoon we're meeting in the park just up the road. There isn't a proper pitch, but we can still practise."

By the time Fran, Megan and Saima had to go home they'd printed off (and Becky had cut up) 250 tickets, and made six huge posters. Fran and Annabel, who were both brilliant at art, had drawn the outlines and everybody else had coloured them in. In fact, they'd been so efficient they had time left over for lounging around on the triplets' beds eating jellybeans and listening to some music. Annabel managed to lounge, eat and draw at the same time, and after about quarter of an hour's furious scribbling she waved her sketchpad triumphantly at Katie and Megan.

"Look!"

Everyone obligingly peered over, craning their necks to see what she'd drawn – a couple of girls in smart purple shorts and lilac shirts with some kind of badge on.

"Cute!" said Megan, grinning.

"Mmmm," agreed Katie. "What's it for?"

"Duh! It's a design for your kit, dimwit! I think it's really cool."

"Mmmm," said Katie again, more doubtfully this time, and darting a "help me!" look at Megan and the others. Saima didn't seem to see any problem, and Becky and Fran were just giggling, very unhelpfully.

"What?" Annabel demanded, sounding cross. "Don't you like it?"

Megan smiled in a peacemaking kind of way. "We do like it, lots. It's just . . . not very practical," she finished in an inspired rush, looking relieved.

"Exactly!" Katie nodded furiously. "Lilac would get really dirty, Bel. After ten minutes on our field we'd just be brown. And it's a bit, um, girly?"

"But that's the point! It's kind of like saying, 'Yeah, we're girls, and we're still way better than you!' See?" Annabel looked disappointed with her sister, and Katie pulled out her last card.

"We do see what you mean, Bel, and it would be cool, but I think we're going to have to use Manor Hill colours anyway – green and red. Maybe you could do us some green and red ones?"

"Green and red?" Annabel put more disgust into the words than Katie would have believed possible. "Oh, I *suppose* so. But honestly, *how* boring?"

Chapter Eight

The triplets slept in on Saturday morning. Katie was exhausted by all the practising and the matches the team had been fitting in, and Becky and Annabel were just keeping her company... Annabel still hadn't got over her disgust at green and red football outfits, but she brought her sketchbook down to breakfast (when Mrs Ryan had finally tempted them out of bed with the offer of beans on toast for a sort of brunch) and started doodling some more designs while holding half a piece of toast in her left hand, dangerously close to shedding its load of beans all over her drawings.

A hand reached out and removed the dripping toast from hers.

"Hey!" Annabel was woken from her semi-thoughtful, semi-just-sleepy haze.

"We said green and red, Bel, not green, red and *beans*. Watch it!"

"Oh. Can I have it back? I was eating that."

Katie rolled her eyes and pointedly put the toast back on Annabel's plate instead of into her outstretched hand. Annabel rolled her eyes back in a frighteningly identical gesture, then grabbed the toast and shoved it all in her mouth at once, making a "so there" face at Katie which didn't go well with stuffed-to-bursting cheeks.

"Bel!" said her mother reprovingly. "Don't you dare spit that out now. Swallow it and behave." She watched beadily as Bel gulped down the huge mouthful. "OK. What's the plan for the rest of the day then?"

"Practising," mumbled Katie, through quite a lot of toast. "This afternoon."

"Mmm," agreed Becky. "I'm going too – going to meet Fran and Feathers and watch. It's in the park." She waved a hand vaguely in the direction of the ceiling, but Mum understood she meant just down the road.

"Can you talk yet?" Mum enquired of Annabel, who beamed at her in a showing off a lot of non-occupied teeth way. "Yup."

"So are you going as well?"

Annabel gave Becky a sidelong look. Their scrapbook plan was already off to a good start. Dad had e-mailed back on Thursday morning sounding anxious.

From: dryan@fostermarcus.co.uk
To:Superstar.3ryans@mailserve.com

Hello loves,
I know what you mean - I'm worried
about her too - Katie hasn't sounded
too happy recently, even though
she's really excited about the team
doing so well. I think the e-mail
scrapbook idea sounds brilliant,
and I can't wait to see everything.
I'll talk to your mum next time I
phone too, she's probably noticed
the same thing. Good luck keeping it
all a secret from Katie!
Love Dad

Annabel had got a couple of good photos of Katie practising in the garden, but this afternoon the plan was to tell Katie that they were bringing the camera to take photos of Fran's dog, Feathers, but actually to get some good shots of the whole team training together. . . "Yes. Can I borrow the picnic rug, please?"

"You can't have a picnic in October," objected Katie.

"I could if I wanted! But I'm not, I just think it would be nice to put the rug down near where you're practising and lie there and watch you all running about like mad things."

"That's so mean." Katie was disgusted. "And I wouldn't do it anyway, because if you do we'll all accidentally-on-purpose kick the ball at you."

"Spoilsport."

"Lazy little so-and-so."

"Excuse me!" Mrs Ryan broke in. "Katie, go and get dressed. Annabel, clear the table, and stop being so grumpy, the pair of you."

Becky smiled smugly at both her sisters, and was rewarded with glares. She went on calmly finishing off her beans on toast, until Annabel attempted to whip the plate from under her nose.

"Hey, I haven't finished!" Becky yelped.

Mrs Ryan turned round from the sink where she was scrubbing beans out of the pan, and gave them a Look.

"You did say to clear the table," protested Annabel, full of injured innocence, but the Look only intensified, and she gave Becky back the plate, muttering about how unfair everybody was.

By that afternoon the atmosphere had calmed down quite a bit, mostly as the triplets woke up properly and stopped sniping at each other. Annabel had been sitting on the stairs, staring vaguely at her French homework (she was quite good at French, but not because she liked it very much, more because she was terrified of her French teacher). Giving up, she wandered down into the kitchen to find Becky playing with Pixie and looking out of the window. Annabel giggled as Pixie pounced viciously on the piece of string and whipped it out of Becky's hand.

"Where's Katie?"

Becky nodded her head towards the garden and Annabel peered out of the window. "Oh, what? She's practising for her practice?"

"Uh-huh. I know we want her to be busy, but she's going a bit over the top, I reckon. I don't feel like telling her though."

Watching Katie's fierce expression of concentration as she guided the ball round the stones she'd laid out on the patio, Annabel agreed. "It's nearly time to go though, I don't reckon she'll mind us telling her that."

But Katie had obviously worked it out for herself. She carefully put the stones back on the edge of Mum's flower border, and came inside.

"Are you two ready? We should go."

"Mm-hm."

They grabbed jackets, Annabel made sure she had the camera in her bag, and they yelled "Bye, Mum!" up the stairs to Mrs Ryan, who was in the study on the computer.

By the time they got to the park Fran and Feathers were already there, and the big Golden Retriever raced up to them excitedly, bringing Fran with him – she didn't have much choice.

Annabel stepped back behind Becky, and grinned at Fran. "It's not that I don't like him, it's just that this is clean and I don't fancy pawprints all over it." She smoothed down her lilac skirt complacently.

Becky was wearing some jeans that could do with a wash anyway (she knew what Feathers was like) and had no such worries. "Hello gorgeous! Aren't you lovely?" She rubbed his ears all over and reduced him to a state of moaning happiness.

"He loves you!" Fran laughed admiringly. "Come on, let's go and sit on that bench. He's been dragging me all over the park for the last twenty minutes, so I reckon he's probably OK to sit down for a bit now."

The three of them headed for the bench, and Katie went over to the small knot of girls who were doing stretching exercises and arguing with Sarah about how they should organize the practice session. Megan wasn't there yet, and Katie was surprised when Cara spotted her and gave her a relieved sort of smile, before very quickly wiping it off and looking the other way.

She supposed it was hard for Cara – the Year Eights didn't talk to her much, and Megan and Katie didn't want to either. Still, she decided firmly, remembering Cara's nasty comments, one half-smile didn't make her any less of a cow. Grovelling apologies would be needed before she was restored to human status. Megan and a couple of others dashed up, and they started the practice, piling up jackets and sweaters for everyone to dribble round.

Becky, Annabel and Fran watched contentedly – it was fun seeing other people working hard – and chatted. After a while Feathers started to whine pathetically, he was desperate to go and join in and he could think of much more interesting things to do with a ball than kicking it in silly patterns.

"Ssssh, Feathers!" soothed Fran. "We've got a job to do. Did you bring the camera?"

"Yup," said Annabel. "Just arrange yourselves so it looks like I'm taking photos of you, but I can actually get the others in instead."

Meanwhile, Katie was enjoying herself. Practising was hard work, but it was fun, and concentrating on her football was how she was trying to keep herself cheerful. The night before, after the others had gone home, she'd worked out loads of really useful training ideas to suggest for today, and clever new plays they could try out. Then she'd looked down at her diagrams in disgust – she was doing exactly what Cara had accused her of! Trying to take over! Sarah was the captain, and she had to be in charge, however hard Katie found it. She'd torn up her notes, and now she was determinedly keeping her mouth shut.

Luckily Sarah had plenty of good ideas of her own – she started off by splitting the squad up into smaller groups to work on passing, and anticipating what the person passing needed them to do – so that they didn't have to waste any time when defenders could be nabbing the ball off them. After a few more exercises, they played a seven-a-side game that was really fun – it was good to see how people on your own team played when you weren't on the same side!

After that they were all pretty worn out, so they pulled on jumpers and fleeces and sat down on the grass to chat for a bit.

Sarah was in a confident mood. "That was a really good session," she said seriously. "Don't you think so?" she asked looking round at everyone. There were nods and murmurs in response.

Then Lizzie, the Year Eight girl who'd been a sub for the semi-final, asked, a little bit sulkily, "Who chooses the team for this match? It's not an official school thing, is it still going to be Mrs Ross?"

Sarah looked surprised. "Yeah, I'd have thought so, why?"

Katie looked at Lizzie, and the glances she was exchanging with Michelle and Caroline, and knew *exactly* why. Lizzie was thinking that if Sarah was choosing the team, she wouldn't pick Katie and Megan and Cara, she'd go for girls in her own year. Suddenly, some of the fun went out of the afternoon – it was like they were Year Eights and Year Sevens again, instead of being a football team. But then Sarah surprised her.

"I *know* that last year when we were in Year Seven we only ever got to be subs, but Mrs Ross'll pick the team, and she'll pick the people who've played best recently, in practices and matches – whoever they are."

And she looked round at everybody in a way that made it perfectly clear what she meant – no more snide comments about the "little ones". It was great! Lizzie just stared at the grass looking cross.

Everybody started to wander off home after that, and Katie and Megan headed over to the bench where the others were restraining Feathers from chasing after everybody.

"That was brilliant, what Sarah said!" Megan exclaimed happily.

"Absolutely," agreed Katie, "and I bet after the semi-final you'll get to be goalie, you were really good."

"I hope so," said Megan seriously. "It would be awful to miss the final after getting to play on the off-chance like that. Anyway –" she checked her watch – "I'd better go. Dad's coming to pick me up outside the park any minute. See you on Monday!"

And she dashed off, waving to the others, leaving Katie to trail her way slowly over to the bench, exhausted.

Chapter Nine

After they got back from the park, Katie flaked out on the sofa. Annabel and Becky looked down at her sternly. "You seriously need to slow down," Becky told her.

"If you keep going like this you'll be dead before Friday," Annabel added. "And then what use will you be?"

"And why are you worrying so much anyway?" asked Becky. "I mean, the boys' team have got *Max*! You're guaranteed to win."

Katie grinned wearily. "I suppose so. But they've just been such pains, 'specially Max – I couldn't *bear* it if they beat us."

For the rest of the weekend the pair of them watched her like hawks, pouncing on her whenever she looked like she might be about to do something energetic, and by Sunday evening she admitted that although she could quite happily kill them both, she did feel less worn out.

Annabel and Becky kept the "Cheer Up Katie" campaign going all week, and tried to stop her doing too much as well. They did all her chores for her, and basically made sure that she was relaxed and in tip-top condition for Friday and Saturday's matches. Annabel even took to timing Katie's practice sessions in the garden and forcibly dragging her back inside after twenty minutes (and a couple of sneaky photos, the e-mail scrapbook was going brilliantly).

By Friday afternoon, both teams, and anyone who was friends with them, were practically gibbering with excitement. The staff were fairly understanding, although Mr Hatton did lose patience in French, which was first lesson after lunch. The two teams and their supporters had been facing off at each other in the dining hall for most of the lunch hour, and French was far from the first thing on their minds.

"Right." It was the second time Mr Hatton had found Max and Ben hissing insults at Megan and Katie. "You four! And whoever else is involved in this ridiculous game – out here!"

Katie, Megan, Cara, Max, Ben and David slunk out to the front.

"Anyone else? No? OK. Now, obviously football is the only thing you can think about at the moment, but at least you're going to do it in French."

There was an audible groan from somewhere in the middle of the classroom, and Mr Hatton whipped round like a snake. "Did I ask for comments? Who was that? Amy?"

Amy looked flustered. It *had* been her, and now she had no idea what to say. The rest of the class watched, feeling glad that it was Amy getting one of Mr Hatton's famous telling-offs rather than them. Besides, Amy was so stuck up, it was fun seeing her taken down a peg or two.

"Not a football fan?" enquired Mr Hatton silkily.

Amy flushed pink and shook her head.

"And you disapprove of my choice of subject for French conversation this afternoon?"

Amy shook her head again, very hard this time, as if to indicate that she wouldn't dare.

"Good. Well then, this will be an opportunity for you to increase your vocabulary, you can come up here too."

Amy crept up to the front to join the others, glaring at Katie and Megan who were smirking at her, and avoiding Cara's eye. Then Mr Hatton dragged the seven of them though a tortuous conversation about their favourite football teams (Amy didn't have one), and then on to that afternoon's match. That was where it got more fun, because Amy pretty much dropped out, and the others insulted each other for a good five minutes – it turned out that French was a very good language to be politely horrible in, and Megan and Katie managed to work out some really choice phrases for Max's football skills. He was scarlet in the face by the time Mr Hatton let them sit down.

Afternoon lessons had been shortened a bit, and the two teams had last lesson off to go and change. Annabel tried very hard to convince Mrs Travers that she and Becky didn't need to go to Geography either, as they were the official girls' team cheerleaders, but she wasn't having any of it, and she cruelly proceeded to ask Annabel a lot of really difficult questions about the different bits of volcanoes.

Meanwhile, Katie and Megan and the others were in the changing rooms, psyching themselves up, with Mrs Ross's help. She seemed to have complete confidence in them, which was great, but Katie found it a little bit scary at the same time – she didn't want to let Mrs Ross or any of the others down. Looking at Megan, she could see that she felt the same way. Mrs Ross had told them all in their practice on Monday that the team for this match, and for the final tomorrow, would be the same team that had played at the semi-final. Michelle, Lizzie and Caroline had looked furious, but what could they say? Katie and Megan had been playing really well recently – and so had Cara, although Katie hated to admit it.

Mrs Ross was striding up and down the changing room. "Just remember, girls. You've trained harder than the boys have, you've been a much more successful team so far this term, *and* you've got more team spirit than they have. You've really got something to prove – they just want to make you look stupid."

Sarah nodded. "We really deserve to beat them, and we can. And just think of the money!"

She was right – they'd sold two hundred tickets, so even if they didn't win, with the extra money from the school they'd raised £400 – which Mrs Ross assured them would be plenty. Katie suddenly remembered what Annabel had stuffed into her hand at breakfast that morning – nerves had made her forget it up until now.

"Sarah?" She was feeling a bit anxious – was she being too pushy?

Sarah turned and beamed at her. "Are you OK?"

"Yes, I'm fine, I just wondered – is it OK to show everybody these? My sister did them." And Katie waved the big pages from Annabel's sketch pad under the captain's nose.

"Wow! Hey, look everyone – Mrs Ross, look! These are great!"

They were Annabel's new designs for the girls' football strip – in green and red. Dark green shorts with a red stripe down the side, and green socks with a stripy turnover top. The shirts were green, too, with red collars, and a red band round the arms and the hem. Annabel had done lots of extras, as well, like caps and team jackets. "For when they raised some more money," she'd said.

Everyone crowded round exclaiming at how cool they looked, and Sarah asked Mrs Ross, "Have we got enough money for something like this?"

Mrs Ross peered at the drawing again. "Yes, I think so – it's great, Katie. Did Annabel do this?"

Katie nodded, feeling very proud of her ditzy sister.

"Excellent. Well, that's what you're playing for, girls!"

Everyone suddenly sobered up. For a minute they'd forgotten about the match in the excitement about their own team strip – but it wouldn't be enough just to have the money for the strip if they lost – it had gone far beyond that now!

Someone knocked on the door, and Mr Anderson's voice called, "Ready, girls?"

This was it!

The girls hugged each other, and hastily murmured stuff like "good luck" and "let's get them", before jogging out to the pitch. The boys were coming out at the same time, and there was a massive wave of cheering. Katie spotted Annabel and Becky standing with Saima and Fran, although standing wasn't actually accurate – they were all jumping up and down and screaming. Even Annabel had stopped pretending she couldn't care less about football – for the moment anyway. She was clutching the digital camera, poised for loads of photos for their scrapbook. Katie waved excitedly, and then went to take up her position. Her nerves had totally gone now, and she was just looking forward to the game, eager to get going.

Quarter of an hour later, the match was properly under way, and both teams were playing well. Annabel and Becky and the others were watching with their hearts in their mouths – the girls simply had to win this! At the moment it just wasn't clear which team had the edge. The boys seemed to be a bit faster, but lost out on accuracy, while the girls' passing was excellent, and they tended to keep possession once they'd got the ball.

But suddenly, everything changed. David managed to do a bit of clever doubling-back that completely wrong-footed Cara, and he was off, whooshing up the field, panicking the defenders, passing to one of the Year Eight boys when Katie tackled him, getting the ball back perfectly – and scoring. The supporters on the boys' side of the field went mad, and all the girls' team could hear was "Losers, losers!" in a massive chorus. All the boys were smirking, and Cara looked like she might cry, especially as a couple of the Year Eights were giving her dirty looks like it was all her fault. They weren't exactly looking friendly towards Megan either.

Katie wasn't able to do much more for Megan than grin sympathetically at her, but just for a moment, she forgot that she couldn't stand Cara, and really felt for her – she could imagine just how she was feeling. She dashed over and gave her a quick hug round the shoulders, a bit awkwardly – hugging one of your worst enemies *did* feel a bit weird. "That was really bad luck. Come on, it doesn't matter, let's get them back."

Cara looked grateful, and muttered, "OK."

The game restarted with the girls extra-determined, desperate to catch up. *We're only one–nil down,* Katie kept telling herself, *that's nothing.* But it seemed an awful lot when every time she looked at one of the boys he was grinning his face off. The boys seemed to have been galvanized by David's goal, and the rest of the first half was very much theirs; the ball stayed up their end with the girls' defenders working manically, and Megan grimly scanning the field while she moved from foot to foot, keeping ready for another shot at goal. All the girls' team were grateful when the half-time whistle went. The game was not going well, and they needed some time to regroup. They trudged off the field, trying not to let their heads hang, while their supporters made an effort to cheer encouragingly.

Back in the changing room, Sarah was trying to cheer everyone up, especially Megan and Cara. "Look, we're only one goal down – we can't give up now, there's the whole second half. We've got to go out and get them! Come on, we *can't* let them win."

Katie was sitting next to Megan, trying not to let her

dwell on her missed save. "It was just one of those things – don't let it get to you, honestly."

Megan grimaced. "I know that really, but I'm still furious with myself." She sighed.

"OK, girls, you need to get up and move around," Mrs Ross warned. "If you stay flumped like that and then leap up and go into the second half your muscles will seize up. Come on, gentle stretches!"

Everyone moaned, but they knew Mrs Ross was right. Katie started off with her favourite exercise, actually one that Annabel had taught her from dancing – you let your fingertips brush the ground, and then uncurled your spine really slowly so that eventually you were standing up. It was one of the nicest ways to warm up or cool down she knew.

The girls marched grimly out on to the field at the end of half-time – there was no way they were going to let the boys get away with this. They went on to the attack the moment the whistle blew, fighting tooth and nail for the ball, and not giving the boys a chance to get themselves going. Looking at the way the boys seemed to be totally gobsmacked by this suddenly fierce team,

Katie reckoned they'd probably spent most of half-time kidding around and sneering at the girls, convinced they were going to grind them into the dust in the second half with no trouble at all, and they'd completely lost their focus.

It still took a good ten minutes of tussling with the boys' strong defence to get anywhere, though. Katie, Sarah and Cara felt like they'd been running backwards and forwards for hours by the time the first decent chance came up, and the tension wasn't just on the field. Becky and Annabel were sure they could sense the waves of frustration radiating from Katie, and they were practically biting their nails (well, Becky was, Annabel wouldn't do anything to damage hers, but she did *feel* like biting them).

The boys' supporters were equally stressed, almost more so because they'd all seemed convinced this would be such an easy win, and now the girls were creating all the decent plays, leaving the boys just firefighting.

Suddenly the ball was free, and Cara was unmarked. She came storming down the field, hotly pursued by

Max and a couple of Year Eight boys. Katie dashed forward to intercept – she could see Cara was running out of energy. Cara passed her the ball, the boys made the classic mistake and switched their attention to Katie, leaving Cara free to catch her breath and get into position. The girls had practised this in the park, and it was going perfectly. Katie and Cara ran in parallel, Katie passed the ball neatly round the boys – and Cara was free to score!

The girls went mad, on and off the field, yelping with delight, hugging each other, everyone piling on Cara, who was practically buried under the rest of the team telling her how brilliant she was – and then they started on Katie.

It took the ref, one of the other PE teachers, Mr Siva, to get them back in the game. "OK, everybody, that's enough for now. Still quarter of an hour to go."

The girls were really excited now, and playing almost like one person. But now the boys were desperate to regain their lead – it seemed to be a stalemate. Neither side would give an inch. Everyone was trying to create decisive plays that would break out of what felt like a deadlock, but they were going nowhere.

Until Max decided to take matters into his own hands.

He knew deep down that he hadn't played particularly well so far – in fact Mr Anderson had told him at half-time that he needed to be making a lot more effort – and he was blaming it all on Katie. They'd been fighting for the last two weeks (well, for the whole term, but particularly since this match had been dreamt up) and he was desperate to get even after all the things she'd said. He was also desperate to win.

He headed down the pitch. Perfect Little Miss Ryan had the ball – good. Katie saw Max approaching, and tensed up. He was heading for her like a charging bull, and there was something very ugly in his face, something that made her feel scared, despite the fact that it was only stupid Max, whom she'd been teasing all term. Suddenly Katie began to realize that Becky might have been right when she said it wasn't a good idea. . . But there was no time to do anything, he was coming up on her so fast.

Becky gripped Annabel's sleeve. "Look at him! Oh no – he's going to do something awful, I can tell!"

Annabel stared in horror – there was nothing they could do – except then she had a sudden brainwave. If Max was going to foul Katie, there *was* one way she could help. She was still holding the camera, and it was a pretty good one, with a mini-video facility – fifteen seconds' worth. And that might be just enough to catch whatever Max was playing at.

Max was on a mission. It was simple, a sliding tackle, a crucial "misjudgement" of the distance, skid and – yes! She was down. Max was at least bright enough not to make too big a deal of his remorse, as he knew no one would swallow it. He concentrated on injured innocence instead.

Katie was just injured. She'd seen the vicious triumph in Max's eyes as he ploughed into her instead of the ball, and she knew that this was revenge, plain and simple. Sitting on the ground, clutching her right leg, she couldn't stop the tears coming, much as she hated to give Max the satisfaction of seeing her cry. Becky and Annabel, not even stopping to think if it was

OK, dashed on to the field, and threw themselves down beside her, just as Mrs Ross stormed up, looking furious.

"Katie! Are you all right?"

"Of course she's not!" burst out Annabel angrily, not caring that she was talking to a teacher. "Look at her, it's her leg. Mrs Ross, do something!"

Katie was curled over, cradling her right leg, leaning on Becky, who was holding her. She could feel this wasn't just a bruise. She knew she wouldn't be able to get up and finish off the match, her leg really hurt, as though she'd torn a muscle. And then suddenly the realization hit her. Max hadn't just put her out of *this* match. If her leg was really as bad as it felt, then his moment of vindictive anger had just destroyed Katie's chances of being in tomorrow's match too. The league final – the match that she had been working for, and looking forward to, the match that she'd been so disappointed that Dad would miss. Well, now it was OK that he was in Egypt – because it looked like she wasn't going to be at the final either.

Chapter Ten

Mr Siva, the referee, was having a massive go at Max. He seemed to have seen exactly what had happened, and was totally refusing to believe Max's protests that it had all been an accident. "Nonsense! You went straight for her, it was totally obvious."

Mr Anderson was equally furious. "What on earth made you do something so stupid? Well, you needn't think you're going to get away with it. You're banned from at least the next two matches, and then we'll see how your attitude improves. I take it you're sending him off?" he asked Mr Siva, who nodded grimly. "Right, go and get changed. I'll finish talking to you later."

Max slunk off the field, leaving the little party still grouped round Katie. Mrs Ross had been examining her leg, and now, helped by Becky and Annabel, she got

Katie to stand up. It wasn't easy. Katie couldn't put any weight on her right leg at all, and Mrs Ross, who had just as much time and effort invested in the next day's final as Katie and the rest of the team, was looking concerned.

The rest of the players seemed shocked – even the other boys on Max's team looked as though they thought he had gone too far – although Becky, looking round at them angrily, decided that if Max had got away with it they might not have minded. David caught her eye and looked really apologetic, but she glared at him, and he didn't say anything. The girls were gathering round now that Katie was up and moving, asking quiet, worried questions.

"Katie, what happened?"

"It looked like he went for you on purpose!"

"Are you going to be OK?"

Katie did her best to smile, but she wasn't really up to answering.

Mrs Ross, still looking upset and angry, started to lead her off the pitch, murmuring comfortingly, "Don't worry, Katie, we'll go and call your mum. I think it might be worth you going to the hospital to get your leg checked over."

Katie suddenly seemed to wake up. "I can't go! Mrs Ross, no! There's only a bit of the game left, and we're going to get a penalty – aren't we?" She turned to Mr Siva, who was hovering at her elbow – he couldn't restart the game until she was off the pitch and her sub was organized.

Mr Siva was still looking grim. "*Oh*, yes. . ."

"I've got to stay –" Katie looked round at the rest of the girls – "come on, we can't let them get away with that!" Then she seemed to droop slightly – the burst of indignant energy had gone, and she was back to thinking about her leg, and missing the final.

Sarah gave her a determined nod. "Don't worry, Katie – they're so going to regret it. Mrs Ross, who's coming on? Lizzie?"

Mrs Ross looked at Katie, and must have sensed something of her determination, because she gave in. "OK. Becky and Annabel, take Katie over to the side – Mr Brownfield will lend you his camp stool for her to sit on, and ask him if he'll go and phone your mum – she needs to know, Katie! I'm not saying you have to go yet." Then she waved at Lizzie, who'd been hovering with Michelle and Caroline on the edge of the field, looking hopeful.

Lizzie pulled off her fleece and dashed on to the pitch, stopping to pat Katie's shoulder and whisper, "That was so unfair!"

Finally the game got under way again, with a penalty awarded to the girls. The boys were now down to ten players, and Max's vicious trick seemed to have had almost as bad an effect on them as it had on Katie. They were playing with even less concentration than before, making stupid mistakes, and although the penalty was a near miss that had Sarah stomping back to the middle of the field quite obviously cursing herself, it didn't take long for the girls to break through and get back into the lead with a brilliant goal from Sarah. Katie bounced on her camp stool with excitement, and then yelped, making Annabel and Becky look at her anxiously.

"It's OK, I forgot, that's all – I shouldn't have moved."

Two minutes later the final whistle went, and the boys trudged off the field in disgust, while the girls danced about collecting hugs, and dashing over to fuss around Katie. It was just after that that Mr Brownfield escorted the triplets' mum over to them, looking frazzled. She'd hurried to the school to make sure Katie was OK.

"Katie! What did you do? Oh, sweetie, are you all right?"

"Mu-um! Ssssh!" Katie looked embarrassed.

Mrs Ross hurried over from where she'd been congratulating Sarah. "Mrs Ryan? I'm so sorry about this – I do think it would be good for Katie to get her leg checked out. Hopefully it's just a muscle strain, but you can't be too careful with this kind of thing."

The triplets had to endure a dreary wait in Casualty, with Mum fussing and getting on Katie's nerves. When finally Katie was seen by a doctor, Becky and Annabel had to stay sitting in the waiting room, wandering up and down and buying cups of disgusting coffee from the vending machine.

"Honestly, the people here are already ill!" coughed Annabel, spitting the brown coffee-ish liquid back into the cup. "This stuff is just unfair."

"They're taking ages," worried Becky. "Do you think something's really wrong?"

Just then Katie and Mum came out again, Katie with her leg strapped up and hobbling on crutches.

"Is it *broken*?" asked Annabel in horror.

"No, but it might as well be," said Katie dolefully. "They think I've torn a muscle, and it's going to take weeks to get better."

"Oh, Katie, for heaven's sake!" exploded Mum. Being summoned to school by the headteacher and then faced with all three of her daughters behaving as though the end of the world had come and only they had noticed wasn't having a very good effect on her. Mr Brownfield had sounded so dismayed that Mum had found it hard to believe that Katie hadn't been really badly hurt. As far as she could see, a simple torn muscle was almost the best possible outcome. "I know you're disappointed, but really it's not that bad. You'll be as good as new in a couple of weeks."

"A couple of *weeks?*" Katie sounded as though she couldn't believe her ears. "Mum, don't you get it? The final is *tomorrow*. A couple of weeks might as well be next year for all the use it is."

It was no good. Katie gave up, and pigeonholed her mother as completely and utterly stupid, or just uncaring. The way she felt, her mother ought to have been screaming and tearing out her hair – that might have made her feel as though the disaster was being taken seriously. At least Becky and Annabel were showing the proper attitude – absolute dismay.

"Mum, Katie's been working for this for weeks and weeks," Annabel tried to explain. "Even I was quite excited about it – and you know how I feel about football."

Mum sighed. "Oh, I know. I was just trying to make you all see that it really isn't as bad as it could have been. I mean, if Katie had broken her leg she'd have been out of the rest of the season – there are more matches scheduled, aren't there?"

"Yes, but *this* is the important one!" Katie exclaimed.

Mrs Ryan looked at her normally sensible Katie and realized that now just wasn't the time. "Well, anyway. Let's get you home. I want to ring that Max's parents and make sure they know how much trouble he's caused."

The hospital had recommended that Katie try to walk as little as possible for the moment, so when they got home she lay on the sofa, with all the pillows and duvets and hot water bottles that Becky and Annabel could find. Mrs Ryan just sighed and let them get on with it, they seemed to be enjoying themselves in a macabre sort of way, even Katie. Annabel was behaving as though Katie wasn't long for this world, and adoring the drama, and Becky was treating her sister as if a rather large stray kitten had turned up on the doorstep and needed fussing over. Mrs Ryan had a horrible feeling that when the dramatic excitement of the situation had worn off they were all going to become terribly upset, obviously Katie most of all, and she really wasn't looking forward to it.

Quite soon after they got home, Megan phoned to see how Katie was. She was properly horrified by the news. "Oh, Katie! I was hoping you were going to say they'd given you something to sort it out. I can't believe you won't be able to play tomorrow." She stopped suddenly when she realized she wasn't exactly being tactful, and then added, "I could *kill* Max!" in a vicious tone of voice.

"Me too," said Katie sadly. "Mum wants to phone up his dad and have a go at him, but I'm trying to persuade her not to. I'd rather kill him myself."

"Anyway I'd better go, Katie, my mum's calling me for tea. Look, I'll see you on Monday."

"Uh-uh. I'm coming to watch tomorrow. I'm not missing the final, even if I can't play in it."

Becky and Annabel exchanged glances – they had a feeling Mum wasn't going to be too happy about that. . .

Katie rang off and slumped back on her cushions, looking tired, and when the phone rang again she didn't answer it, even though the portable one was lying on the back of the sofa next to her. She felt too gloomy. Becky, who was perched on the arm of the sofa at her feet, looking at her worriedly, had to reach for it.

"Hello?"

The person on the other end sounded rather embarrassed. "Um, hi, is that Katie?"

"No, it's Becky, who is it please? Do you want to speak to Katie?"

"Um, it's David? From school. Hi. I was just ringing to see if your sister was OK. Er, is she?" David sounded as though he was getting more flustered by the minute, and Becky felt sorry for him. She should have been nicer to him earlier on. She made her voice a bit more friendly as she replied, and Annabel raised her eyebrows at Katie, who was looking intrigued.

"Oh hi. No, she's not really, she's torn a muscle in her leg so she can't play tomorrow, but she hasn't actually *broken* anything."

"Who *is* it?" hissed Katie irritably, feeling that Becky was stealing her phone call and making a vague grab for the phone which Becky easily evaded. "Shall I put Katie on? I'm sure she'd like to talk to you."

"Oh – oh yes, OK." David sounded as though he would have preferred to keep talking to Becky. She vaguely assumed he found Katie a bit scary – some people did. She handed the phone over. "It's David."

"Hi?" said Katie enquiringly.

David was obviously finding it difficult talking to someone that a member of his team had attempted to cripple an hour or so before.

"Hi Katie. I was just ringing to see how you were. And to apologize for that moron. I'm really sorry – it was a good game until then, you played really well. All the girls did."

"Thanks," said Katie, only a little bit grudgingly.

"Um, anyway. I hope you feel better soon. OK? Bye!" And he rang off in a hurry.

"Wasn't that nice of him?" asked Becky in a pleased sort of voice.

"Hmmm." Katie sounded exhausted, and when

Mum, who'd been gently eavesdropping from the kitchen, suggested that she went to bed, she agreed almost without arguing.

The next morning, Katie's leg wasn't feeling any better, and she was having a hard time being sensible and well-behaved about it. It hurt, and the crutches were a total nuisance, and she couldn't stop thinking about the final that afternoon.

Becky stopped hovering around the sofa after Katie had carefully (and obviously) restrained herself from snapping something rude when Becky asked her for the third time in half an hour if she needed anything, and went to find Annabel. She was in their room trying out a very complicated hair braid that was in one of her magazines, but it wasn't going right and she didn't mind an excuse to give up.

"Do you think we should tell Katie about the scrapbook for Dad?" asked Becky, flumping down on her bed. "If she ever needed cheering up it's now."

Annabel looked thoughtful. "Well, it's either going

to make her feel better or loads worse. I think it'll *probably* make her feel good though."

"Mmmm." Becky nodded. "I'll get the printout."

They had been going to give Katie the printout of all their photos and bits after the final, so it was all ready. They'd added the photos and the video of yesterday's match too, and sent them off to Dad, although of course the video just looked like a still photo on the printout. It was still on the camera though. They'd shown it to Mum – it had made her even more determined to phone Max's dad.

They headed downstairs with the sheaf of paper, and peeped round the living-room door. Katie was reading a football magazine, or staring at it anyway. She looked really down, and Becky and Annabel exchanged glances – this was definitely worth a try.

Katie looked up. "I'm OK, honestly! I don't need anything!" she said exasperatedly.

"We've brought you something anyway," said Annabel, grinning at her a bit nervously. "Look." And she removed the magazine and stuffed the printout into Katie's hands.

Katie leafed through it idly, then her attention was caught. She read a few sentences of one of Becky's match reports. "Hey, what *is* this?"

"It's a photo-diary," said Becky.

"Like you get for really famous football players, photos of them when they were little, and stuff," added Annabel. "We've been sending it to Dad."

"Dad's seen it?"

"He thinks it's brilliant, Katie," said Becky, crawling carefully on to the sofa next to her. "He thinks *you're* brilliant."

"He e-mailed this morning, after he saw the latest bits – he wants to tear Max limb from limb. Look –" Annabel brought out the digital camera and pressed the video replay – "you can see why."

Katie watched, fascinated, as Max tripped her all over again.

"How long have you been doing this?"

"Just a couple of weeks. Since you were so upset about him not being there at the quarter-final," explained Becky. "Now that you know about it, it can be much better – Dad wants you to add bits, about

132

what it was all like. He said there's no way it's as good as being there, but it's the next best thing."

When Mum came in to mention lunch, she found all three of them curled up on the sofa, carefully avoiding Katie's leg, and giggling as they looked at the photos – Katie's face tended to be quite funny when she was really concentrating.

Over lunch they explained to Mum what had been happening, and pointed out the best pictures.

"This is great! You two are dark horses, keeping this a secret!" she exclaimed, flicking through it.

Becky and Annabel exchanged smug looks, and Katie looked at her watch.

"I'd better go and get dressed," she said, bolting the last of her toasted sandwich, and grabbing her crutches.

"Dressed?" Mrs Ryan put down the scrapbook pages. "Why, darling? You don't need to, really."

"Mum, I'm not going to school in my pyjamas!"

"School? Oh no – Katie, no. You are not going to watch that match, I'm sorry, but the doctor said—"

"Mum! I have to go! It's the final, I've got to see it –

and if I'm on my crutches and I'm careful, it'll be fine. Please!"

Mrs Ryan glared at her, but she could see how determined Katie was on this, and she didn't really want to stop her – she'd actually behaved amazingly well about her leg, and her mother could just imagine what the fallout would have been if something like this had happened to Annabel. She shuddered. "All right. I'll take you in the car. But we're coming straight home afterwards!"

"Yes! Thanks, Mum!" and Katie lurched round the table to kiss her.

Mrs Ryan smiled grudgingly and turned to Becky and Annabel. "You two, help her up the stairs – we haven't got loads of time."

By the time they got to school the match had already started – it had taken Katie longer than she'd expected to get dressed, even with help. Becky, Annabel and Mum hovered carefully round Katie as she limped her way over to the field. There were lots of parents and friends watching, and Megan's parents made sympathetic noises when they saw the state of Katie. Someone came up next to Becky, and grinned shyly.

"Hello – I was hoping you'd be here – er, all of you, I mean. I, um, wanted to see if Katie was OK," David said awkwardly.

"That's really sweet of you." Becky beamed at him. And then Katie demanded, "How's the match going?" and he went into football mode, and started to explain every step anyone on the pitch had taken so far, as Annabel observed to her mother disgustedly.

After about five minutes Mrs Ross noticed them, and at half-time (with either side yet to score, Katie noted worriedly) she came over. She was beaming, and she greeted Katie delightedly.

"Katie – I'm so glad you came! I really wanted Mr Terry here to have a chance to meet you. He's seen you play a couple of times, and he thinks you might be able to try out for the county girls' squad – he's their coach."

It was one of the few things that could have made up for missing out on the final – to be one of the best players in the county! Katie was so excited that she was completely tongue-tied, but Mr Terry was very nice, and very sympathetic about her leg. He arranged a time with Mum for her to come along to one of their practices, and then they settled down to watching the rest of the match. Katie was so pleased that she could *almost* enjoy watching without being upset that she wasn't playing herself.

Her team were playing so well, it was actually quite fun to have a chance to watch them. Especially as they were playing another good team, St Felix, and the two sides were really well-matched. Megan managed some fantastic saves, and Katie was glad that Mr Terry was still watching. He certainly looked quite impressed.

But it was still nil–nil five minutes from the end, and Katie wondered worriedly whether it would be a penalty shoot-out – poor Megan! But luckily Sarah managed a sneaky goal, practically as the referee was about to blow his whistle, and just when the other team were obviously starting to think they were going to have to go to penalties and had stopped concentrating quite so hard.

The Manor Hill team were ecstatic, jumping about and hugging each other, and Katie suddenly felt really miserable again. OK, things had turned out a lot better than she'd expected from today, but she still wasn't part of *this*. Then Sarah and Megan rushed over and grabbed her. The referee had produced a very impressive-looking silver trophy from somewhere and Mrs Ross was waving at them to line up. She grinned as she saw Katie there too. The whole team were given medals on really smart stripy ribbons, and then the referee invited the team captain to come and get the trophy. Sarah started forward, and then came back and put her arm carefully under Katie's.

"Come on! You *so* should have been playing, come and get it with me!"

They snail's-paced up to the referee, and everybody cheered when they eventually got there. Katie looked round, grinning, and saw Becky and Annabel jumping up and down like mad things in-between taking yet *more* photos, and Mum smiling proudly. Dad wasn't there, but thanks to Becky and Annabel she knew he was thinking about her, and missing her too. They'd won! She couldn't wait to get home and tell him. Maybe she hadn't been able to play, but suddenly Katie felt it didn't matter. Everyone was hugging her, as though she was a heroine.

"Well done, Katie!"

"Are you feeling OK?"

"Did you see that save just after half-time?"

"When can you play again?"

And someone with curly brown hair in bunches was hugging her a bit gingerly, and saying how good it was she was there. Katie smiled at Cara – she had a feeling this truce wouldn't last long once they were all back at school on Monday, but just for the moment, it didn't matter!

Don't miss:

Triplets

Becky's Problem Pet

Becky can't believe it – Jack, one of her classmates, is breeding rats . . . as snake food! She's determined to put a stop to it; she's just got to work out how. Annabel and Katie want to help, but just the thought of the rats' long pink tails and sharp teeth has Bel squirming with horror!

And that's not the triplets' only problem – their arch-enemy, Max, is stirring up trouble. Luckily, it's nothing a bit of match-making can't solve, but should Becky let Bel play Cupid?